Irritated by a re... currently seeme... ...control over, Aimi favored him with a long-suffering look.

"You're wasting your time, you know," she told Jonas bluntly, keeping her voice down. "I'm not going to take the bait, however attractive the lure."

One eyebrow rose mockingly. "How many times did you have to tell yourself that last night?" he taunted, and she drew in a sharp breath.

"Once was enough. You're not that irresistible," she shot back equally mockingly, and Jonas laughed appreciatively.

"You know, you're supposed to cross your fingers when you lie like that," he cautioned, never taking his eyes off her for a second as she approached. Breathing normally was no easy matter for her at the moment, and she wasn't used to that.

She would have to try harder. Much, much harder. Bad enough that he was occupying her thoughts—she could not allow him to tempt her into breaking the solemn promise she had made. She had to resist.

AMANDA BROWNING is still happily single and lives in the old family home on the borders of Essex, England. She enjoys her extended family and is a great aunt to eighteen nieces and nephews. She especially enjoys her twin sister's two grandchildren, and she risks serious damage to her back when playing the fool with them!

She began writing romances when she left her job at the library and wondered what to do next. She remembered a colleague once told her to write a romance novel, and she went for it. Her first effort elicited an invitation to visit Harlequin® headquarters. Although her first two manuscripts could not be used, the third was accepted, and she hasn't looked back since.

Besides writing, which occupies a great deal of her time, she is very interested in researching her family tree. This has led to discovering relatives in the United States and Canada, and just recently these relations have visited the U.K. She is about to plunge into the world of the Internet in order to make more discoveries, which should be interesting in more ways than one!

What is left of her spare time is spent doing counted cross-stitch, and she really enjoys the designs based on the works of Marty Bell, as well as the gorgeous designs of Victorian Ladies, angels by Lavender & Lace and Mirabilia ranges—they are so intricate. She finds it very satisfying to finish one and finally see it hanging on a wall.

Of course, she still manages to find time for some gardening. Like most gardeners, she is constantly waging war against cats, who think the beds are their private toilets, and the snails, who dine out on her flowers. So far she has resisted the ultimate deterrent of trekking out at night with a torch and a bucket, but she's giving it serious consideration!

JONAS BERKELEY'S DEFIANT WIFE

AMANDA BROWNING

~ THE BILLIONAIRE'S CONVENIENT WIFE ~

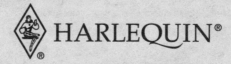

HARLEQUIN®

TORONTO • NEW YORK • LONDON
AMSTERDAM • PARIS • SYDNEY • HAMBURG
STOCKHOLM • ATHENS • TOKYO • MILAN • MADRID
PRAGUE • WARSAW • BUDAPEST • AUCKLAND

Recycling programs
for this product may
not exist in your area.

ISBN-13: 978-0-373-52712-0
ISBN-10:   0-373-52712-8

JONAS BERKELEY'S DEFIANT WIFE

First North American Publication 2009.

Previously published in the U.K. under the title
THE BILLIONAIRE'S DEFIANT WIFE.

Copyright © 2008 by Amanda Browning.

www.eHarlequin.com

Printed in U.S.A.

JONAS BERKELEY'S DEFIANT WIFE

CHAPTER ONE

SOMETIMES the world could change in an instant. One moment everything was exactly the way you planned it to be, and the next it had become a place you barely recognised. This was how it was for Aimi Carteret that sultry summer evening, and it was the second time it had happened in her sometimes turbulent life.

Just moments before the second cataclysmic event that was to cause such havoc occurred, she was sitting at the large dining table of Michael and Simone Berkeley, enjoying the friendly banter. Beside her sat their son Nick, a man of genuine warmth and kindness. He was a renowned surgeon, like his father, and his father before him. Opposite were Nick's sister Paula and her husband, James Carmichael.

Six months ago Aimi had been employed by Nick to organize his hectic life. Besides operating, he had lecture tours, guest appearances on all forms of media, and had even begun to compile a family history. She worked from the study in his home, but did not live in. That was something she never did. Her work and her private life never overlapped.

Not that she had much of a private life, but that was by choice. Her life had changed dramatically nine years ago, and the mad social whirl she had enjoyed to the fullest had been left behind and never regretted. Guilt had sobered the outrageous teenager, and she had vowed to turn herself into someone she could be proud of.

She had thrown herself headlong into studying history at university, but making a career out of it had been hard. So she had learned all the skills she needed to become a personal assistant, and had been temping for a high class agency ever since. Coming to work for Nick had allowed her to use her grounding in history, and help him with his research. She had, after much hard work, found a niche for herself where she was able to feel a degree of peace.

If her old friends could see her now, they would barely recognise her, Aimi thought to herself. She didn't wear make-up, when once she had used it to enhance her large green eyes, always kept her shoulder-length blonde hair smoothed into a pleat at her nape, and pre-ferred smart suits and casuals to modern fashions.

When she had been at university, she had even worn glasses. Plain glass, of course. They had been a ploy used to keep people at a distance. She had been at university to work, not play. Her playing days had ended with a tragedy she would never forget. All she had wanted to do was blend into the background and be left alone.

It seemed strange now to remember how outra-geously she had once flirted with the opposite sex. Having inherited her looks from her actress mother, Marsha Delmont, Aimi had had no trouble attracting men, and had enjoyed their company, but she had never taken them seriously and never had any deep relationships with any of them. Her life had been about having fun, but after Austria and the terrible events that had happened there, that had all ended. She had spent the years since proving she could be a person of value.

Her life was the way she wanted it. She was here in her official capacity as Nick's assistant, but his parents had welcomed her into their home in the country as a friend. The plan was for her to look through the books and papers in the study for relevant material for Nick's book, but all Nick's family would be coming to a barbecue tomorrow, for their annual bank holiday weekend get-together, and he had insisted that she join in the festivities.

Sitting at the table, listening to the conversation, sometimes taking part, she was glad she had agreed to come. This was how normal people behaved with each other, and it was a poignant reminder for Aimi, who had once thought endless shopping, wild, glamorous parties where drink flowed like water and everything was loud laughter and music was the only way to live. That Aimi would have considered this deadly dull, but the Aimi of today bitterly regretted that she hadn't wised up sooner. Such was the benefit of hindsight. It showed you what might have been, and damned you with the knowledge that you could never go back.

In those final few minutes before her world would be knocked off its axis and sent spinning into space for a second time, everyone was laughing at something Paula had just said. Aimi found it so funny, her eyes were watering and her stomach ached. It was as she was using her napkin to wipe her eyes that the distant chime of the front doorbell permeated the room.

Simone Berkeley looked at her husband in mild query. 'I wonder who that could be,' she said to the room at large.

'Were you expecting anyone, Mum?' Paula asked, only for her mother to shake her head.

Moments later, they all heard the sound of footsteps coming towards the room and everyone looked expectantly towards the door. It opened seconds later and a tall, dark-haired man stepped into the room, grinning at the sea of faces.

'I hope you left something for me, you pack of gannets!' he exclaimed cheerfully, and his remark was met by cries of delight.

'Jonas!'

The family immediately leapt to their feet as one, leaving a bemused Aimi to swivel round in her seat and examine this late arrival. She had heard of Jonas Berkeley, of course, the oldest son, who owned a high-powered company and lived a jet-set lifestyle which took him off to all corners of the globe. His name was often in the newspapers, sometimes for his work, but more often for the latest woman in his life. Naturally he had an open invitation to the family gathering, but nobody had expected him to be able to make it. Hence their surprise and delight.

Her own surprise was her response to him, which was totally unexpected. The instant she laid eyes on him, something stirred in the depths of her. All her senses appeared to leap to attention, as if her whole being recognised and responded to something in him. His laughter as he greeted everyone sent shivers down her spine and the rakish sparkle in his startlingly blue eyes dried her mouth.

For all her wild youth, Aimi had never actually experienced such a blatantly physical response to anyone in her twenty-seven years. She was suddenly made very much aware of the blood pulsing through her veins and the rapid beating of her heart. All at once her smile faded away and it was then, as Jonas Berkeley glanced from one member of his family to another, that their gazes locked.

She could actually see the moment when he was stopped in his tracks, and her heart lurched anxiously. Something elemental forked through the air between them, only to be broken when his sister claimed his attention, yet there had been time enough to see the predatory gleam which had entered his eyes. Shocked and disbelieving, Aimi turned away, pressing a hand to her stomach.

Oh, my God, she thought dazedly. What had just happened? Silly question, Aimi, you know darned well! She had just experienced the pull of an immensely strong sexual attraction, and her whole body was quivering as a result. It was the very last thing she had expected, for she had worked hard to keep the attractive, outgoing side of her nature under control—to be the complete antithesis of her former self in every way. Which was why she had eschewed all forms of romantic entanglement. No man had ever made her control slip.

Until just now, that was. Without a word he had broken through her defences, making her feel things she did not want. She didn't know why it had happened now, only that she had to make rapid repairs so the damage did not show. Telling herself to be calm, she breathed slowly until she felt in control again. Now she should be able to give the appearance of calmness, although in reality she was still trembling inside.

A hand touched her arm and she jumped, looking up to find Nick beside her.

'Come and say hello to my brother. I'm eager for him to meet you,' Nick invited, and Aimi's heart fluttered anxiously at the thought of looking into those amazing eyes again so soon. However, there was one little part of her that needed to check out if it had really happened or if she had imagined it, so she smiled, as if the ground hadn't just rocked, and stood up.

As she took the half a dozen steps to where Jonas Berkeley stood within the circle of his family, Aimi had the weirdest sensation that she was walking down a pre-destined path. A momentary sense of caution whispered, *Go back*, yet a stronger force kept her moving. She couldn't stop her eyes from rising to meet his and, the instant that happened, once again the air seemed to become positively charged, making it difficult to breathe properly.

'OK,' Nick declared, noticing nothing amiss, and made the introductions. 'Aimi, this strapping fellow is my brother, Jonas. Tall, handsome and disgustingly wealthy, he's also a bit of a Casanova, so you have been warned. And this young woman is my indispensable assistant, Aimi.'

Jonas's teeth flashed white as he smiled directly into her eyes and held out his hand. 'Hello, Nick's indispensable Aimi. I'm very pleased to meet you,' he greeted her in a voice whose low timbre was an unexpected delight to her ear.

Aimi gasped silently, more than a little unnerved to know she was still feeling the full force of the man's charisma, despite her hasty repairs to her defences. He oozed supreme male confidence and sexual allure, and it was stunning. Knowing she was not as cool as she would like to be, she hesitated fractionally before taking his hand, and knew she had been right to do so when his fingers closed around hers. The contact sent a wave of tingles up her arm and throughout her system, causing the tiny hairs to rise. Her faint start was absorbed by his hand, which tightened on hers momentarily.

'I'm pleased to meet you, too,' she returned politely, glad to hear that she at least sounded normal. Easing her hand free, she coiled her fingers into her tingling palm. 'Nick talks of you often.' It was true, though he had never said what a charismatic man his brother was. Probably because he never saw him that way. Women would see a whole different side to him. A side she would have preferred to remain in blissful ignorance of! Whilst she might admire a man's looks aesthetically, she tried to never allow herself to be moved by them. Today, though, something was going badly wrong and she didn't like it.

'Ah, that would be the reason my ears have been burning lately,' Jonas joked lightly, his mouth tweaking into a boyish grin. 'So, how long have you been working for Nick?' he asked and, as he did so, his eyes took in the grey pencil skirt and white blouse she was wearing, despite the stifling summer heat. There was a quizzical glint in his eye when he met hers again.

'Six months, give or take,' Nick informed him, smiling at Aimi. 'I tell you, everyone could do with an assistant like her!'

His brother looked from one to the other. 'Is that so? Do I detect more than just a working relationship here?'

he enquired, and Aimi got the distinct impression that it was not an idle question. He wanted to know just how involved his brother was.

Nick laughed and shook his head. 'Good Lord, no! Nothing like that! She's brought order to the chaos of my life. Isn't that right, Aimi?'

'I do my best,' Aimi agreed uncomfortably, wondering if Nick realised he had just as good as told his brother she was not off limits. From the wry amusement in Jonas's eye, he knew it, and knew that she did, too.

'What made you decide to visit this weekend? Did you find yourself between women?' Nick asked with a surgeon's precision, and Aimi had to stifle a sudden urge to grin.

Jonas raised a lazy eyebrow at her, ignoring his brother, and smiled. 'Delicately put, Nick, as always. I did happen to find myself with an unexpectedly free weekend. But I don't think it's going to be as disappointing as I first thought!'

Fully aware of what he was implying, Aimi's eyebrows rose. She might not play the field any more, but she hadn't forgotten how the game was played. 'Oh, I'm sure it will be,' she insisted, smiling back coolly.

His head tipped. 'You think so? Funny, I usually find something to keep me amused.'

Nick snorted. 'Typical Jonas! Don't you think it's time you grew up? You're thirty-four. You should be looking to settle down and start a family.'

'I'll leave that to you. I'm happy with my life the way it is.'

'At least I'm looking! You just keep dating those beautiful airheads! What on earth do you see in them?

You can't even have an intelligent conversation with any of them!' Nick insisted doggedly.

'Shame on you, Nick!' his sister broke in on what appeared to be an old argument. 'Jonas can date whatever sort of woman he likes. Just because he's bound on cutting a swathe through the female population doesn't mean he won't settle down eventually. He'll do that when he's good and ready.'

Jonas sighed in the face of such heavy-handed criticism from his nearest and dearest. 'Thanks for making me sound like a heartless Lothario, Paula.'

Paula quickly pressed a kiss to his cheek. 'Of course you're not heartless, but you *are* a Lothario. I love you, Jonas, but I have to admit you have a cavalier attitude towards women that stinks. What you need is to fall in love with a woman who doesn't want you for a change!'

'That's my girl,' Jonas exclaimed dryly. 'I wouldn't expect anything less of the sister who waded into a brawl to rescue her little brother!'

'Oh, yes, she saved me all right!' Nick responded aggrievedly. 'Then launched into me for getting into a fight in the first place!'

Everyone laughed at that, and Aimi was relieved the focus of attention had passed on to someone else.

'Come along, everyone. Let's sit down again before our dinners get cold,' Simone Berkeley chivvied them back to the table. 'Jonas, you sit next to Paula. I want to hear all about what you've been doing lately.'

Moments later a place had been laid and a full plate set before him. Back in her own seat, Aimi discovered, much to her chagrin, that Jonas was now sitting directly opposite her. It meant it was impossible not to see him whenever she raised her head. Even looking down, she was vitally aware of him. His presence in the room was an energy her errant senses registered in minute detail. Ignoring him was simply out of the question and her eyes had a will of their own, watching him from under her lashes whilst she ate. Thankfully, he chatted away with his mother so she was able to study him with a certain amount of freedom.

The first thing she noted was how black his hair was, then the strong set of his jaw. Yet his lips spoke of sensuality. She wondered how they would feel, and immediately wished she hadn't as a delicious shiver swept over her. Aimi closed her eyes and took some more steadying breaths. She had to get a grip, and as quickly as possible. She prided herself on her cool demeanour and needed it to be working perfectly. It would never do to let Jonas see he could affect her in any way.

From what she had just heard and seen, she knew the man didn't need any extra encouragement when it came to attracting moths to his flame. However, he was going to find this particular moth had an impermeable heat shield. He might have a reputation for going through women like a hot knife through butter, but not this one. She was simply not available.

Opening her eyes, Aimi felt her confidence strengthening. She was not a weak woman, at the mercy of her senses—she was stronger than that. Bolstered, she was about to eat more of the delicious food on her plate when she felt the hairs on the back of her neck stand to attention. Her nerves skittered and, unable to ignore it, she glanced up to find Jonas watching her, the look in his eyes highly provocative.

Their gazes locked for a fleeting moment before Jonas smiled knowingly and looked away. It was long enough, however, to set her heart pounding. She chose to believe it was from annoyance, ignoring the small voice that wanted to say differently. Nor did she have to ask herself why he had looked at her like that, for she knew the answer. The man was no fool, and had sensed her initial response to him. But that moment was gone. She would not let anything slip again.

With her mind settled on that point, she raised her head again and began taking an interest in the general conversation, just as she had before Jonas had arrived. Once or twice she caught his eye, seeing mocking amusement there, but she was alerted now and didn't react to it. Finally, after the strangest hour Aimi could ever recall spending at a dinner table, the meal was over.

'Let's have coffee on the terrace,' Simone suggested, dabbing her napkin against her throat. 'Maybe there will be a breath of air out there. It's so hot, it's positively stifling!'

The country had been in the grip of a heatwave for some days now, and it didn't look like ending any time soon. Naturally, the whole family were only too happy to go outside, where looking down the garden towards the ornamental lake made them feel cooler immediately.

'You must be glad to get out of the city this weekend, Aimi,' Michael Berkeley remarked as he handed round the coffee his wife was dispensing.

Aimi took her cup with a wry smile. 'Oh, yes! Though my apartment is air-conditioned, on nights like these it doesn't seem to make a difference. Working in your study will be much better than in some musty old archives.'

'I thought you were my brother's assistant. Are you moonlighting as an archivist?'

The question came from Jonas, and Aimi steadied herself before turning to him. It was just as well she did, for she discovered he had made changes to his appearance since eating dinner. He had removed his jacket and tie, loosened the top buttons of his shirt and rolled up his sleeves, which gave him a totally different look. In his suit he had been suave and very much the international businessman; like this he looked ruggedly male and quite stunningly sexy.

It all registered on her senses and, after what had happened just a short time ago, it didn't really surprise her that her mouth went dry. Fortunately she had the foresight to take a sip of her coffee to moisten her lips before answering him. 'I'm not moonlighting. I'm helping with the research for Nick's book.'

'Nick? That doesn't sound very professional to me,' Jonas goaded, and Aimi smiled faintly.

'You might be the type of employer who insists on formality, Mr Berkeley, but your brother prefers a friendlier atmosphere,' she replied coolly, and he grinned appreciatively.

'Call me Jonas. I never insist on formality here,' he declared, and Aimi realised she had not helped herself. Now she would have to call him by name, or look a fool. 'So you're a researcher as well.'

'She's good at it, too,' Nick immediately piped up in her praise. 'Not surprising when she's got an honours degree in history.'

Jonas inclined his head towards Aimi in a gesture that showed he was duly impressed. 'A multi-talented woman. No wonder Nick snapped you up. If history is your first love, why aren't you working at one of the museums or institutes?'

'Unfortunately, those kinds of jobs don't come along often and, as I've become used to eating three meals a day, I had to do something else,' she informed him smoothly.

'So, history's loss is my brother's good fortune,' Jonas returned, equally smoothly. 'And ours, too, of course. Otherwise we would not have had the pleasure of your company this weekend.'

'You'll see very little of me, I'm afraid. I'm here to work,' Aimi pointed out, mighty glad to be able to do so.

Jonas looked surprised. 'Surely Nick doesn't intend to keep your nose to the grindstone whilst the rest of us party?' he challenged, giving his brother a disapproving stare.

'Of course not. Aimi knows perfectly well I expect her to relax, too,' Nick came back promptly, and she smothered a sigh of exasperation.

Jonas smiled, and his eyes were dancing. 'I shall make it my business to see that she does, then.'

Aimi could feel her spine tense at the suggestion, and it took all her effort to keep her expression calm. 'Don't bother,' she refused politely, to which his smile broadened.

'Oh, it's no bother. It will be a pleasure.'

The only sign of her annoyance was a brief flaring of her nostrils. She knew she could not make any further protest, but would make sure to avoid him wherever possible. Meanwhile, she caught sight of the amusement in his eyes and felt compelled to respond.

'What line of work are you in, Jonas?' she enquired, finding it curiously hard to make his name emerge naturally. 'Or have you made so much money you don't need to work?' she added, referring to what Nick had said when introducing them earlier.

He seemed to find that amusing. 'I buy up ailing companies and try to improve their health,' he answered simply, and she frowned at the caveat.

'What if you can't?'

Jonas smiled and, because it was totally natural and free of mockery, it lit up his face, causing Aimi to catch her breath yet again at the twinkle in his eye. 'Then I break them up into saleable parts.'

'Making a tidy profit on the way,' Nick added. 'Remember me telling you he was disgustingly rich?'

It sounded good, but Aimi could see a flaw. 'Making money is one thing, but what about the people? The workers? What happens to them if your cure fails?'

Jonas didn't appear in the least annoyed by being asked to justify his actions. 'They stay with the company wherever possible. This is about turning a company around, changing bad management into good. If everything goes well, everyone wins. When I have to break one up, we do our best to find alternative employment within our group. Does that meet with your approval, Aimi?' he queried sardonically, and Aimi nodded, smiling wryly.

'Of course. If I sounded disapproving, it's because not everyone in your line of work has a conscience,' she returned calmly. 'I apologise if I was rude.'

His lips twitched and now the gleam was well and truly back in his eyes. 'There's no need. You were only saying what many others think. However, it's good to know there's something about me you find attractive.'

Now that had her eyes flying to his, her lips parting on a tiny gasp of surprise. The bold challenge, right in front of his family, knocked her off balance, as did the sardonic amusement glittering in those blue orbs that dared her to respond. However, Aimi was not given to running away. Taking a breath, she moistened her lips, and her senses rocked when she saw his eyes follow the movement. Then his gaze lifted, and for a vital second the irony was gone and she could see heat there. Scorching. Elemental. Of course, as soon as he saw she had seen, his lips twitched, and she knew she had been played by a master. Which gave her all the more reason to reply.

'Are you fishing for compliments, Jonas?' she taunted with gentle mockery, and laughter erupted around her.

'Sounds like it to me,' James Carmichael interjected. 'That has to be a first!'

Everyone started teasing him, which he took with remarkable fortitude, an attitude which she *did* find attractive—amongst other things. She had always liked a man with a sense of humour and the ability to laugh at himself. Yet that changed nothing. She was not interested in whatever games he had in mind. Sitting back in her seat, she withdrew from the fray and concentrated on drinking her coffee.

The gentle ribbing continued for some time, until Jonas changed the subject. 'How many are coming to the barbecue this time?' she heard him ask his mother, but the answer was lost, as she took the opportunity to regroup her thoughts.

Aimi recognised that she was dangerously close to getting caught up in the miasma of the senses that was sexual desire, and she found that unsettling. From the moment she had vowed to change her life, no man had registered on her radar. In the beginning she had been too haunted by what had happened to feel anything but, as the healing process had gone on, she had turned the radar off deliberately. She hadn't wanted to be attracted to anyone, to find happiness in a loving relationship, for it deepened her sense of guilt to feel so alive. So well had she done the job that she had thought her defences were impermeable, but a few moments in Jonas's presence had destroyed that belief. Even now it went on. Unseen, Jonas called to her and the whole of her being responded. It was so strong, even the hairs on her skin stood to attention. The sheer intensity of it was staggering.

She didn't want to feel it, didn't want to be so aware of him, but her body wasn't obeying the rules. All she could do was try to block it out as best she could. Once the weekend was over, that would be the end of it.

She tuned back in to the conversation in time to hear Paula announce that she and her husband were going for a walk around the lake if anyone was interested in joining them.

'I could do with a walk,' she said, jumping at the chance, and looked at Nick. 'Will you join us?'

'Paula will only nag me if I don't,' he pretended to grumble as he stood up, and his sister poked her tongue out at him.

Aimi braced herself to hear Jonas declare his intention to join the group, but it didn't happen and she let out a tiny breath of relief. Though she forced herself not to look round, she could feel one pair of eyes on her back as they walked away.

It was marginally cooler down by the water and she and Nick strolled along, side by side, enjoying each other's company, following the other couple. Eventually Paula and her husband disappeared around a bend, leaving her and Nick alone momentarily.

'It's much better here,' Aimi declared, thankful for some respite from the heat—the tangible one and that given out by a pair of fathomless blue eyes.

'Jonas and I used to play on the lake when we were kids. We built a raft and would pretend we were ship-wrecked sailors. Of course, we weren't allowed to do it until we could swim. Jonas had different interests then,' he added somewhat pointedly, making her look at him.

'What do you mean?' she couldn't help but ask, and Nick rolled his eyes.

'That was before he discovered girls. Tall ones, short ones. Blondes and brunettes. All of them beautiful, and all of them madly infatuated with the handsome devil. He's never had to fight for a woman in his life. They take one look at him and, wham, they topple into his arms like ninepins! It's all too easy. He'll never settle down. Why would he, when he can have any woman he wants?'

Aimi had known the moment she had seen Jonas that he would be a hit with the ladies. She shivered inwardly as she thought again about the instant reaction she had experienced. 'No wonder you call him a Lothario!'

Nick laughed. 'He doesn't treat women badly. On the contrary, he's generous to a fault. He just never gives anything of himself. It's all purely physical. He's my brother, and I wouldn't wish him harm, but he could do with falling hard for someone, just to learn a lesson.'

'Not everyone wants to settle down,' she ventured,

knowing that such a situation was not on the cards for her. Once she had envisioned herself with a husband and children, but that dream had vanished a long time ago.

Nick came to a halt and, when he turned to her, she could see the frustration he was experiencing. 'Of course not. It isn't that. Jonas has lived a charmed life. Everything has come easy to him. He needs a reality check. Basically, he needs to know he's human like the rest of us.'

'You mean he needs to suffer,' she proposed, smiling just a little, and Nick grinned, an action that heightened the resemblance between the two brothers.

'Sounds awful, doesn't it? It's going to take someone pretty remarkable to do it, that's for sure.'

Aimi sighed as they began to walk on. 'I'm not sure you should be telling me all this,' she remarked uncomfortably, but Nick shook his head.

'On the contrary, you're the one who most needs to know,' he declared, bringing her head round in complete surprise.

'I don't see why,' she refuted, wondering what he could mean.

Nick tutted in a rather parental fashion. 'Of course you do, so just you remember what I told you when the pressure gets turned up.'

She glanced round at him curiously. 'Whatever do you mean?'

This time Nick favoured her with an old-fashioned look. 'Aimi, you're a beautiful green-eyed blonde, and Jonas isn't blind. Be careful.'

Aimi was both alarmed that he should realise what his brother was doing, and warmed that he cared enough to warn her. Yet he need not have worried. 'I'm afraid your brother will be wasting his time. I have no intention of being his entertainment for the weekend. Thank you for caring, though.'

'I wouldn't want to see you hurt,' he told her, and she smiled wryly.

'I won't be, because I don't plan to get involved with him,' she added reassuringly.

'I'm sure that's what most of his conquests said,' he countered with a grimace and Aimi stopped walking and looked at him.

'Please don't worry about me; I'm going to be fine. I've known men like your brother before, and I'm immune to them.' It was almost true. Jonas, however, was a different kettle of fish, and he had taken her by surprise. He wouldn't do so again.

Nick studied her face, and what he saw there convinced him he could relax. Maybe she was right, and she was immune. She certainly had defences like he had never seen. 'I'll say no more, then,' was all he said, and they continued on their way.

CHAPTER TWO

IN HER bedroom later that evening, Aimi pushed the windows wide to gather in what breeze there was, but the warmth already trapped inside her room made her feel hot and sticky all over again. Kicking off her shoes, she reached up and removed the pins that held her hair in place and the blonde locks tumbled in waves over her neck and cheeks. It felt good to let it loose, but tomorrow it would go back up again, reinforcing the look she had worked hard to maintain over the years.

In the mirror she could see the natural waves of her hair softening her features, making her look vibrantly young and alluring—carefree almost. It sent out a message that jarred on her nerves. She wasn't that person any more. Would never allow herself to be her again. It was part of her self-imposed penance.

Turning away from her reflection, she walked into the bathroom to take a cooling shower. Feeling marginally better, she dried herself on a fluffy towel and slipped into a thigh-length silk nightie. Turning off the light, she stretched out on top of the bed. However, it proved impossible to sleep, and not just because of the heat. Alone in the humid darkness, time passed slowly and her thoughts inevitably travelled back to that moment when she had first seen Jonas. She could visualise the sheer power and magnetism of him. Just thinking about it set her nerves tingling.

'Damn!' she exclaimed in exasperation, shooting up into a sitting position. 'Stop it, Aimi!' Yet for once her brain refused to obey. It played over the look in his eyes when their gazes had locked, and once again heat swept over her with such stunning force that her stomach muscles clenched in reaction.

That had her scrambling off the bed and padding to the window to draw in deep gulps of warm air. Yet it didn't help. The memories were too powerful. Too stunning. When she closed her eyes, she could almost feel the brush of his gaze on her lips as her tongue sought to moisten them, and she groaned helplessly.

'For heaven's sake, Aimi, get a grip!' she muttered to herself. 'You're not going to do this! So what if the man oozes sex appeal? You cannot allow yourself to be drawn into the flames. He's a playboy. All he wants is a body in his bed, and that isn't going to be you!'

Aimi dragged a hand through her damp hair and sighed. Lord, it was hot! Even the water in the shower had been tepid. She longed to feel something cool against her skin and, with sudden insight, knew just where she could find it. Moments later, she had slipped on her silk robe over her nightie and was padding barefoot down the stairs, the robe flying out in her wake like the wings of an exotic bird. Her destination was the large modern kitchen, and she was relieved to find she had it to herself when she passed through the door, closing it behind her. There was no need to turn on the light, for the moonlight gave the room a silvery glow.

It took a few minutes of quietly searching through drawers and cupboards before she found what she was looking for—a napkin, which she took to the counter beside the larder-style combined refrigerator and freezer. There was a delicious blast of coldness when she opened the freezer door, seeking out the bag of ice cubes. Taking a handful, she wrapped them in the napkin, closed the freezer and sat down at the table, sighing with pleasure as she drew the ice-filled napkin over her skin.

They were moments of pure bliss and she almost purred as she wondered why she hadn't thought of this before. Propping her feet on another chair, she hummed to herself as she lazily cooled herself down. Which was why she was miles away when the abrupt sound of someone tapping on the window made her almost jump out of her skin.

Her head shot round and, to her complete surprise, she saw Jonas standing outside the kitchen door.

'Oh, my God!' she gasped faintly, suddenly aware of the picture she must make, sexily draped over two chairs and wearing next to nothing. Her instinct was to rush off, but he was gesticulating to the door, clearly wanting to come in. There was nothing else she could do but put a brave face on it and comply. With a grimace of dismay, she set her napkin of ice down and padded over to the door to let him in, holding her robe together with one hand.

'Thanks,' he said, the moment he was inside, locking the door again. 'I thought I was going to have to sleep on the lawn,' he added with wry humour, which faded when he turned and looked at her standing in the moonlight, seeing her state of dishabille properly for the first time.

'Now that's a sight I don't see every day!' he breathed seductively and with obvious pleasure, whereupon Aimi hastily tied the belt of her robe and folded her arms as his blue eyes roved over her, causing her body to respond in a way he would easily recognise. She was as mortified as it was possible to be to have been caught this way. When he finally looked her in the eye again, there was a wicked gleam in the blue depths and a sensual curve to his lips. 'Were you expecting me? I hope so—you definitely have my attention,' he queried in a voice that vibrated along her nerves like the purr of a contented cat.

'Naturally, you would think that!' she shot back instantly, finding it incredibly hard to keep her composure. She felt unusually edgy and ill at ease. 'It was hot, so I came down for some ice. I didn't expect anyone to be about at this time of night. What were you doing out there?'

Jonas drew a hand through his hair, ruffling it rakishly, and she had to stifle a groan as the way he looked registered on her senses. She wondered if it was a calculated move or pure happenstance. Whatever, the effect was the same.

'Like you, trying to cool down after a hotter than expected evening,' he responded with more than a dash of irony. 'I went down to the pool soon after you went off for your walk, and fell asleep. I was trying the doors and windows, and that was when I saw you, draped across the chairs, wearing that provocative bit of nothing.'

'You should be thankful I was here; otherwise you would have had to stay outside,' she told him with all the firmness she could muster. 'And my clothes are perfectly respectable,' she added for good measure, which drew a rakish laugh from Jonas.

'Oh, I'm thankful all right, and there's nothing wrong with what you're wearing. You look good in it, and that's the problem. How the hell am I supposed to sleep now?' he charged sardonically, eyes gleaming flirtatiously.

Her heart lurched in sudden anxiety because the same thought had occurred to her. 'You shouldn't say things like that to a family employee. It's hardly appropriate,' she returned swiftly, determined to keep the moral high ground at all costs.

The moonlight made it easy to see the way one of his eyebrows rose mockingly and the sardonic twist of his lips. 'Drop your arms, Aimi, and we'll talk about appropriate behaviour,' he taunted, and Aimi felt heat scorch her cheeks at the knowledge that he had seen her body's response to him before she could hide it.

She watched speechlessly as he walked to the table and opened up the napkin of ice she had been using. Taking a cube, he rubbed it around his neck as he turned to look at her.

'That was a caddish thing to say!' she exclaimed in an attempt to sound outraged, and he laughed unrepentantly.

'I'm sure my brother just got through telling you I am a cad!'

Aimi immediately came to Nick's defence. 'He did no such thing!'

Jonas didn't look as if he believed her. 'Really? Remind me to thank him the next time I see him,' he said mockingly, allowing his gaze to roam over her from head to toe. Propping himself against the edge of the table, he crossed his feet and grinned provocatively. 'You know, that bit of nothing you're wearing leaves just enough to the imagination.'

Aimi drew in a ragged breath, knowing she ought to be able to handle the situation, yet finding it hard to remain aloof. This was the heat Nick had been talking about. It was pretty potent, and the sanest thing would be to get out of the kitchen. 'This is pointless,' she said shortly. 'I think we should just go to bed.'

Something wicked flashed in his eyes. 'Now that's really cutting to the chase!' he drawled sardonically, and she kicked herself for choosing her words badly.

'I didn't mean it like that,' she corrected hardily.

'However tempting the prospect might be, hmm?' he murmured softly and in the quiet of the night the words echoed like thunder, sending shockwaves through her system.

'You have some nerve!' she gasped faintly, and Jonas laughed seductively.

'I think you *should* go to bed, Aimi, before the need to know undermines your resolve,' he advised.

To say she was unsettled would be an understatement, and it made her respond in a way she never would have otherwise. 'What resolve?' she queried rashly, and Jonas shook his head and sighed.

'You know already. I'm talking of your resolve to have nothing to do with me,' he answered softly. 'That was the conclusion you came to during your walk, wasn't it?'

'God, you're arrogant! My resolve to have nothing to do with men like you was made years ago, not this evening,' she declared scornfully, and he looked amused.

'Men like me?'

Her eyes narrowed as she looked him up and down, doing her best to make it obvious she found him wanting in every department. 'Men who think they can have everything and everyone they want, just by asking. I have nothing but contempt for you.' It wasn't strictly true, but she was fighting a rearguard action here.

'If that is the case, why do you respond to me?' he asked softly, pulling the rug from under her feet.

Aimi held on by the skin of her teeth. 'I do not respond to you.'

That produced a soft laugh. 'I could prove you wrong, but it's late and we're both tired. I suggest you go upstairs now. We'll continue this fascinating conversation tomorrow.'

'We'll do nothing of the sort!' Aimi shot back tautly.

'By the way, I love your hair like that. You should wear it loose more often. It's very feminine, very sensual,' Jonas declared in the next instant, and her hand immediately rose to touch it.

Aimi realised she had forgotten all about it; having him see her with her hair down was like an invasion of privacy. Feeling more vulnerable than she had for many years, Aimi decided she had had enough and that a dignified retreat was in order. However, as she went to walk past him on her way to the door, her foot hit a wet patch on the tiles and slid out from under her. With a gasp of shock, she flailed around for something to hold on to and suddenly found herself caught by a pair of strong hands and hauled in to Jonas's powerful chest.

'Easy. I've got you,' he declared into her hair, but she scarcely registered him for her senses, now that she was safe, were being bombarded by the heady male scent of him, combined with the solidity of his powerful chest. It was a sensory overload that had her tipping her head and looking up at him through stunned eyes.

Jonas met that look and, though his eyes gleamed hotly, his mouth curved with wry humour. 'I think what you're thinking right now is highly inappropriate for a family employee,' he declared ironically, pushing her upright but not letting her go.

Dismay washed over her as she realised just how totally she had betrayed herself in that one gesture. What she wanted to do was run away from those knowing eyes, but what she did was tilt her chin at a belligerent angle. 'Keep your hands to yourself,' she commanded bitingly, shrugging him off, and walked away. It was hard not to hurry to the door, but she managed it and went out without a backward glance.

Out in the hall, breathing raggedly, she stared at the closed door. She had just made a complete fool of herself. To find herself experiencing an unwanted attraction to the man was one thing. To let him see it, quite another. Something about him just kept getting through her defences, and she didn't like it. Not one little bit.

Aimi berated herself all the way up to her bedroom, where she spent a restless hour trying to sleep. Before sleep finally claimed her, however, she had promised herself that she would keep well away from Jonas for the remainder of the weekend. It shouldn't be hard to do, as she was here to do research. She doubted very much if he was the type to spend much time in a library. A harem, maybe, but not a place full of musty books!

One thing was certain—no matter what he thought,

she was absolutely not going to be the next notch on his bedpost! She had worked too hard for too long to achieve this level of peace with herself to surrender it now.

The new day dawned as hot and humid as the last. Though she had managed to get some sleep, Aimi didn't feel the least bit rested, for Jonas had invaded her dreams, haunting them with tantalising possibilities. It seemed as if, waking or sleeping, she was being pulled by her senses into dangerous waters, and the current was incredibly strong. The man was too attractive for his own good, and it didn't help to remember how he had broken through her defences with incredible ease.

As she took yet another lukewarm shower, she considered the situation a little more logically. What had really happened, after all? She had discovered she was powerfully attracted to a man and that he was attracted to her. That didn't mean she was going to fall into his arms! Jonas might be an extremely attractive man, but she had known a lot of attractive men before and been able to resist them! But since that awful day she hadn't looked at a man with interest and, with a strength of purpose she hadn't been aware she'd possessed, she had simply shut down those feelings and emotions. So Jonas was going to be out of luck. She had come here to work, and that was all.

Taking comfort from that thought, she stepped out of the shower and dried herself off. Choosing what to wear wasn't a problem; she had packed only the bare essentials. Two skirts and a few blouses. Nick had told her to include a swimsuit, which she had done, but she did not expect to wear it. Today she chose her cream pencil skirt and a pale blue short-sleeved silk blouse. She slipped her feet into comfortable shoes and swept her hair back into its pleat with the ease of long practice. Smoothing the material of her skirt over her hips, she examined the view in the mirror. She looked cool, efficient and out of reach—just the way she liked it.

She was twitching her skirt into place when there was a knock on the door.

It was Nick, and he smiled as he stood in the doorway of her room. 'Good morning, Aimi. You're looking amazingly cool,' he greeted her, and her eyes crinkled as she laughed wryly.

'I don't feel it, I assure you,' she observed lightly, reaching up to sort out the collar of his polo shirt, which had gone awry.

'Well, just looking at you makes me feel cooler,' he returned charmingly, and she sighed, shaking her head.

'Nick, Nick, you're almost as bad as your brother! You must have gone to the same charm school,' she declared, grinning at him, totally unaware of anyone approaching.

'Morning, Nick,' Jonas greeted his brother and, when Aimi gave a start of surprise and glanced round, he nodded to her, lips curving into a provocative smile as he ran his gaze over her like a caress. 'I like the skirt, Aimi, but, all things considered, I prefer what you were wearing last night,' he said with a soft laugh before walking on.

She stepped back from Nick, feeling her cheeks grow warm. His remark, innocent-sounding as it was to anyone else, immediately brought back memories of what had occurred in the kitchen last night.

Nick frowned at his brother's retreating back. 'Hey, what did that mean?' he called out after him.

Jonas didn't miss a stride as he threw his answer back over his shoulder. 'You'd have to ask Aimi,' he advised, and jogged down the stairs.

Nick turned to her, eyebrows raised. 'What did he mean? You weren't wearing anything fancy last night. Have I missed something?'

She winced, knowing where his thoughts were going. 'Your brother was referring to later on. He had been locked out, and I just happened to be down in the kitchen when he was looking for a way in. That's all.' Looking at him, she saw the sceptical expression he was wearing and sighed. 'I happened to be in my nightie and robe.'

Nick let out an exasperated tut. 'Aimi, I warned you to be careful. He's my brother, and I love him, but when it comes to women…'

She squeezed his arm reassuringly. 'I know, but give me some credit. I'm not going to fall for his line of charm. I came here to work, and that's all,' she reassured him. Last night was a mistake which wasn't going to happen again.

Nick pulled a wry face and sighed. 'Sorry. I'm just a bit over-protective. You work for me so I feel you're my responsibility. I won't have Jonas playing his games with you.'

Aimi was warmed by his caring, but he didn't need to worry. 'Don't worry. Let's go down to breakfast and afterwards you must show me the library.' Working had always been a good way to distract her thoughts.

They followed in Jonas's wake, entering the breakfast room together, to find it empty. Maisie Astin, the housekeeper, was just bringing in fresh coffee and hot croissants to set out on the sideboard.

'Good morning!' she greeted them brightly with a cheery smile. 'Everyone has been eating outside today. Help yourselves, and let me know if you need anything else.'

'Thanks, Maisie. What would you like, Aimi?' Nick asked as he picked up a plate.

'Some of Maisie's melt-in-the-mouth croissants and coffee sounds perfect,' she decided, exchanging smiles with the other woman, who disappeared back into the kitchen.

'I'll bring it out. You go find a shady spot,' Nick ordered, leaving Aimi with nothing to do but wander outdoors.

Of course, then she wished she hadn't because the only person at the table was Jonas. Had he not looked up, she just might have retreated indoors again, but, as if some invisible sensor had alerted him to her presence, his head came round and he looked directly at her.

'Deciding whether it's safe to join me or not?' he challenged sardonically, and Aimi was compelled to walk forward.

'Not at all,' she denied blithely, smiling as if nothing had passed between them mere hours before. 'I was just enjoying the view.'

His lips twitched. 'Ditto,' he responded, and the lazy meander his eyes took as they ran up and down her body told her his view had nothing to do with the garden. It caused her heart to skip a beat and her nerves to start tingling as if he had actually touched her.

Irritated by a reaction she currently seemed to have no control over, she favoured him with a long-suffering look. 'You're wasting your time, you know,' she told him bluntly, keeping her voice down, not wanting Nick to hear. 'I'm not going to take the bait, however attractive the lure.'

One eyebrow rose mockingly. 'How many times did you have to tell yourself that last night?' he taunted, and she drew in a sharp breath.

'Once was enough. You're not that irresistible,' she shot back equally mockingly, and Jonas laughed appreciatively.

'You know, you're supposed to cross your fingers when you lie like that,' he cautioned, never taking his eyes off her for a second as she approached. She was so conscious of it that breathing normally was no easy matter, and she wasn't used to that.

Having reached the table, Aimi dropped on to a chair opposite him. 'Contrary to what you might think, I'm not in the habit of telling lies,' she corrected, feigning an ease she was far from feeling. Just being near him made her feel tense and unsettled.

Jonas raised that eyebrow again, to good effect. 'Really? Now I would have said most women are natural born liars.'

'That's a huge sweeping statement. Your jaundiced view was caused by a bad experience, I presume,' Aimi declared with heavy irony.

'It's a jungle out there,' he returned with a wicked grin, and Aimi knew that she would never forget that particular look as long as she lived.

'And men aren't liars?' she challenged scornfully, knowing she could name a dozen at least. 'It would be easier to think the moon is made of cheese!'

Jonas relaxed back into his chair, crossing his legs at the ankles. 'Now that sounds like the voice of experience talking. Is he the reason you dress the way you do?'

He was so far wide of the mark that Aimi almost laughed. 'I dress to please myself, not a man,' she was quick to point out.

He looked at her thoughtfully. 'Is that so? Are you trying to tell me nobody ever gets to see the exotic lingerie you wear? That would be a crying shame!'

Memories of those moments in the kitchen last night made her wince inwardly. 'My clothes are none of your business. I would not have gone downstairs had I known you were there.'

'Then I would have had to spend the night down by the pool, and never have got to see you in that mind-blowing confection of silk and lace. It's imprinted on my memory even now.' Jonas shifted, bringing one leg up to prop his ankle over the other knee. 'Seems to me, I know something about you that no other man does. Under that starchy exterior you like to wear satin and silk. What other secrets do you have, I wonder?'

'None that you will ever know!' Aimi shot back curtly but, instead of responding, Jonas merely smiled as he watched her.

'What happened to your hair last night? You weren't wearing it up in the kitchen,' he observed, and her nerves gave a giant leap.

'I don't sleep with my hair pinned up,' she explained calmly, only to see his smile broaden.

'You know what I think, Aimi Carteret?'

'Your thoughts couldn't interest me less!' she retorted witheringly, making him laugh.

'I think you practice to deceive.'

That was too close to the truth for comfort. 'Like I

said, your thoughts are of no interest to me. *You* are of no interest to me!'

'Whilst you are of considerable interest to me,' Jonas countered smoothly. 'I find myself thinking about you all the time.'

'How boring for you!' Aimi said, and he laughed—a sensual sound that sent goose-bumps down her spine.

'Oh, I have the feeling that you will never bore me, darling Aimi.'

The unexpected endearment sent a shockwave through her system, and her breathing went awry. 'I am not your darling.'

'Not yet, I agree,' he conceded, but his assertion didn't make her feel any better.

Goaded, her temper rose. 'Never!'

He looked her directly in the eyes before speaking. 'Ah, you should never say never. I discovered that myself last night. I would have bet good money that I would never find it hard to sleep in my old bed, but last night proved me wrong. I was terribly restless,' he explained with a wicked grin, mayhem in his eyes.

'You can't possibly blame me for that,' Aimi argued, as her nerves responded with a now familiar skitter. It was as if her defences had totally vanished, leaving her open to react to everything he said or did. She didn't understand how they could have abandoned her now, when she needed them most.

'Can I not?' Jonas countered, lips twitching with barely concealed humour. 'You were the one who raised my blood pressure,' he remarked sardonically, taking another mouthful of coffee from the cup on the table.

Somehow Aimi contrived to maintain her cool expression. 'My blood pressure didn't need lowering. I went to bed and slept dreamlessly,' she added for good measure, mentally crossing her fingers at the lie.

'Hmm,' he murmured doubtfully, running his hand over his chin. 'There's more to you than meets the eye.' Aimi merely raised her eyebrows. After a moment Jonas continued, 'Did you know I was supposed to be in America this weekend? Fortunately, the meeting was called off at the last minute.'

'Much to everyone's delight,' she remarked dryly, and something flashed in the recesses of his eyes.

He laughed. 'Nicely done, Aimi. Very tactful. It's no wonder Nick speaks so highly of you.'

'I do my best,' she replied smoothly, not bothered that he recognised what she was doing, just grateful she had the skill to draw upon.

'Ah, here comes the cavalry,' Jonas declared dryly, and Aimi glanced round to see that Nick had appeared with their breakfast. 'Not a moment too soon, eh?'

Nick had overheard that remark and, as he placed her cup and plate before Aimi, he glanced at his brother. 'What's not too soon?' he queried, frowning, and Jonas grinned at him.

'Your arrival with the food. Aimi was getting ready to eat the table.'

'Sorry I took so long,' Nick apologised, and she shot Jonas a warning look.

'You didn't. Jonas is pulling your leg.'

'He has a habit of doing that,' Nick confirmed wryly.

Jonas's lips twitched and he sat up straighter. 'Actually, I was flirting with Aimi, and she was giving me a hard time.'

'Good for you, Aimi!' Nick encouraged her, giving her a wink. 'There are too many women who fall into his arms at a click of his fingers already!' He took the chair next to her and started to wolf down his breakfast. Aimi followed suit, and silence fell over the table.

'What time are the hordes descending?' Jonas asked some time later.

'Midday onwards. Then it's the same old drill. Dad will be doing his usual cremation job on the bangers and burgers!'

Jonas grinned and glanced at Aimi. 'Have you been to one of our beanfeasts before?'

She couldn't help smiling at their amusement. 'No, this is my first,' she admitted. She was a little nervous about meeting the family. Finding herself amidst a group of strangers had been commonplace once, and she had thrown herself into the party mood with enthusiasm. Since that awful day, though, the thought of laughing and having fun had seemed wrong. How could she ever do that again, as if nothing had happened, when she was the one at fault? She couldn't and live with herself, so she had avoided parties, and her so-called friends had slowly drifted away. These days she preferred small, intimate dinners with people she knew well.

'Then you're in for quite an experience!' Jonas told her with droll humour, breaking her introspective mood.

Nick clicked his fingers. 'Hey, do you remember when…'

Aimi tuned out as the brothers took a humorous trip down memory lane. Sitting back in her seat and slowly eating her last croissant, she watched them both closely. They were very much alike. Both were handsome men, but Nick's face had softer lines. His hair was dark brown, whilst Jonas's was black. Nick exuded warmth, gentleness and caring, yet it was Jonas's more rugged lines that drew her attention.

Quite unexpectedly, Aimi found herself wanting to reach out and trace the lines of his face, to commit them to memory. Which was a ridiculous thing to be thinking. She did not want to remember him. The sooner they parted company, the better. Yet, as soon as the thought entered her head, one small part of her suddenly felt lost. She looked down at her coffee cup, frowning in yet more confusion. What was it about him that touched her? Good Lord, he only wanted one thing from her. Yet...there was just something about him.

The sound of laughter made her tune back in and she looked up to see Nick doubled up with mirth and Jonas grinning from ear to ear. It brought a smile to her own lips and an odd twist to her heart.

A piercing whistle cut into the laughter and made all three look round. Michael Berkeley stood at the end of the terrace, beckoning to them.

'Come along, you two! I need some muscle to set up tables. Get a move on!'

With wry looks at each other, the two brothers got to their feet obediently.

'Dad likes marshalling his troops,' Nick remarked fondly.

Aimi grinned at his expression. 'Have fun!' she teased and, as he walked away, caught Jonas's eye. The mocking look was back. As her stomach lurched, she raised an eyebrow questioningly. 'Was there something else?'

'Just this,' he said and, walking round the table, bent

to drop a swift kiss on Aimi's cheek before she could prevent it.

'Hey!' she exclaimed, whilst her pulse did a skittish pitter-pat. The feel of the brush of his lips on her skin took her breath away, it was so stunning.

Jonas was unrepentant. 'I have to have some fun. Consider that a little something on account!' he riposted neatly and followed his brother, leaving Aimi speechless.

She was left watching his rear view, and quite a view it was. Damn the man, he was just about perfect to look at. Broad-shouldered, with slim hips and long, powerful legs. There was no point trying to pretend otherwise, few men could compete with him. Of course, she immediately berated herself for noticing, when she was trying to keep these wanton wayward thoughts about him out of her mind.

She would have to try harder. Much, much harder. Bad enough that he was occupying her thoughts; she could not allow him to tempt her into breaking the solemn promise she had made. She had to resist.

CHAPTER THREE

In an effort to do that very thing, Aimi quickly finished her breakfast, then went indoors to find the library. It was a wonderful room, full of shelves of leather-bound books that called to her. For the next few hours she happily browsed, making notes of the books she wanted to dip into for the information Nick required. Finding a diary written by Nick's great-grandfather, she took it to a chair where she tucked her feet up under her and was soon lost in another world.

Nick found her there much later. 'There you are!' he exclaimed as he entered the room, and Aimi looked up in surprise. She had been so lost in the writing she hadn't heard anything.

'Did you want me?' she asked, hastily sitting up, swinging her legs down and slipping her feet back into her shoes.

'Yes, the rest of the family have arrived. We'll be eating soon,' he told her as she stood up, and Aimi's heart sank.

'Honestly, Nick, your family don't want a stranger in their midst. I'll be much more use to you here.'

'The books can wait,' he said, removing the diary from her fingers and setting it down on a table. 'I want you to have some fun this weekend, too.'

He would not be gainsaid and, without further protest, Aimi allowed herself to be ushered out of the house and into the garden. The barbecue had been set up by the pool, and that was where the family had congregated. Nick introduced Aimi to the various groups around the tables. Everyone made her feel welcome and were genuinely fascinated about the book she was helping Nick to research. In a very short time, Aimi was able to relax and, instead of going through the motions of acting as if she were enjoying herself, was actually doing that very thing. She said as much to Nick when they had a brief moment to themselves.

'My family are good people. I'm glad they've made you feel comfortable.'

Aimi glanced around her, seeing the large group of laughing, happy people through new eyes. It had taken a long time, but today she was discovering that she could actually enjoy herself without feeling guilty. The sky hadn't fallen in, nor the world come to an end. She didn't know why today had proved to be different from all the other days, but for the first time in aeons she had been able to put her burden aside for a few hours and simply live for the moment.

'Thank you for insisting I join you,' she responded with a smile, and Nick gave a tiny bow.

'You're very welcome, I'm sure,' he quipped and, as they moved on, Aimi's heart felt that tiniest bit lighter. Of course it wouldn't last. Later, reality would return, but for now she accepted this strange new sense of freedom without question.

It was while they were chatting to one of his cousins that Nick's beeper sounded. Though it was his weekend off, as a specialist surgeon he was often on call for emergencies.

'It's the hospital,' Nick informed her, recognising the number of the caller. 'I'd better take it inside. I won't be long.' He gave her a rueful look before striding away.

Aimi remained where she was, chatting until the conversation turned to a subject she knew nothing about, and then her attention wandered. She was watching the antics of two of the children when a movement drew her gaze. Her heart skipped a beat when she realised she was looking at Jonas, who was strolling along talking to a much older man.

She knew she ought not to look, but somehow she just couldn't tear her eyes away. He appeared totally at ease, laughing at something the other man said, and the sheer pleasure on his face made her catch her breath.

'That's Great-Uncle Jack,' one of the women at the table said, almost making Aimi jump. She looked round immediately.

'Sorry?'

'With Jonas. He used to be a sailor, and has loads of old yarns about his adventures. The children love him,' the woman explained with a friendly smile.

'Ah, yes,' Aimi murmured faintly, deeply relieved the woman had mistaken the source of her interest. 'I don't think I've met him yet.'

'Then you're in for a treat. Look, we're going to get

something to eat. Are you coming?' the woman invited,
but Aimi shook her head.

'I'll wait for Nick. He shouldn't be too much longer.'

The others wandered off to join the mêlée for food,
leaving Aimi alone for the moment. Of course, she immediately looked for Jonas where she had last seen him, but
the two men were no longer there. No amount of searching brought him into her view again, and her heart sank.
That was when she asked herself just what she thought she
was doing. Had she gone completely insane? This won't
do, Aimi. It really won't do, she castigated herself.

She stood up, deciding to go and join the queue after
all. Anything to take her mind off the wretched man. Yet,
as she turned, she found herself looking straight at him
over a sea of seated people. Before she could move, and
as if he could feel her eyes on him, Jonas glanced round.
Their eyes locked and once more the intensity of the
connection staggered her. This time, though, there was
an added extra. It was a physical pull which silently
urged her to close the distance between them. That blue
gaze seemed to be saying, *I know where you want to be,
and all you have to do is come to me.* Her lips parted on
a sharply indrawn breath, and she saw the upward curve
of his lips as he smiled faintly.

'There you are!' Nick's voice, speaking from right
behind her, caused Aimi to spin round hastily, her heart
thudding like mad.

'Oh, Nick!' she exclaimed, her head feeling alarm-
ingly woozy, partly from shock and partly from what he
had interrupted. 'You scared the life out of me!'

Nick immediately frowned in concern. 'I'm sorry,
Aimi. You were miles away!'

Lord, how she wished she really was miles away! Aimi thought. A million miles from Jonas and the sensual spell he was weaving around her! Maybe then she could think clearly and get off this seesaw she had been riding since she first set eyes on him. He was a temptation she simply had to resist with every ounce of her strength for if she didn't, how could she ever look herself in the eye again? She had failed Lori once; she could not do so again.

Keeping that thought in mind, Aimi made a concerted effort to put Jonas from her mind by concentrating on Nick instead. 'What did the hospital want?'

'They needed to let me know about an emergency case that came in. They might need me to operate, so they wanted to put me on standby. They're monitoring the situation, but it doesn't look good. I should know in a few hours. Sorry, Aimi, but I think I will have to go back tonight.'

Aimi nodded understandingly, for it was the nature of his job. 'Never mind. At least you got the chance to see your family.'

'I knew there was a good reason why I hired you. You take everything so calmly; nothing seems to throw you,' Nick observed with awe. Aimi very nearly laughed at that, for his brother was playing the very devil with her vaunted calm. Unaware of what she was thinking, he urged her towards the tables of food. 'Come on, let's get something to eat. I'm famished, and I don't know when I might get to eat next.'

Aimi allowed herself to be steered away but, as she did so, she couldn't resist taking one quick glance backwards. Jonas was still watching her and she looked away hurriedly, her nerves leaping. Oh, Lord, she prayed silently, please make this weekend go quickly. Before she was tempted into doing something really, really stupid, which would jeopardise everything she had achieved.

Fortunately she was rescued by the massed ranks of the Berkeley family. Once a mountain of food had been eaten, the family got down to the serious business of the afternoon—playing games. It culminated in a form of rounders, with men against women, and created an uproar of laughter, for the rules were informal at best and each point fiercely contested. Aimi found herself laughing until her sides hurt and her jaw ached. It was all good fun and by the time it came to an end in the early evening everyone was exhausted. Gradually the other family members began to drift away again, back to their own homes, and peace descended upon the house once more.

Nobody felt like eating a heavy dinner after all that food, especially with the heatwave still holding sway. Fortunately, Maisie had prepared a light meal of salad and quiche, which she'd left in the fridge before she went home to her own family. There was much teasing whilst they ate a late supper. Contested runs were rerun with plenty of noise and, with very little effort, Aimi was able to concentrate on that, not Jonas, who sat mere feet away. Even though her senses were spine-tinglingly aware of him every second, she was pleased with herself for not showing it.

The meal over, Aimi and Paula volunteered to wash up, whereupon Nick and James agreed to wipe. They had barely done half of it, though, when Nick's beeper went off again. He used the phone in the kitchen to answer it and, from the one-sided conversation they could all hear, it was pretty clear he was going to have to go back to London. When he hung up, one look said it all. Aimi quickly dried her hands and went over to him.

'It's critical now? You must go straight away?' she asked, slipping back into the role of his assistant in an instant. 'Should I clear some of your calendar?'

'I'll let you know about that. Hopefully, it won't be necessary. The thing is, I don't know what to do about you. I need to go straight to the hospital from here, and I won't be coming back. How will you get home?'

'That's not a problem. I'll bring her back with me on Monday,' Jonas declared, and they all turned to discover that he had come into the room silently and was standing just inside the doorway. Aimi's instinctive response would have been a polite refusal, but Nick was too quick for her.

'That's a great idea, Jonas. You can have some extra time here for research that way, Aimi.' He looked at her with a relieved smile which made it impossible for Aimi to disagree, much though she would have liked to.

Resigning herself to spending another two days in Jonas's company, she took a steadying breath and smiled politely at him. 'Thank you. That would be kind of you,' she said, and didn't miss the gleam that came and went in his eyes.

'You're welcome.'

Nick rubbed his hands together, thoughts already on the task ahead of him. 'OK, so that's settled. Now I must get a move on.'

'I'll help you pack,' Aimi declared decisively, following him.

It meant she had to brush past Jonas in the doorway

and, though she tried to stop herself, she could not help but look up at him as she did so. There was a wicked gleam in those blue depths that caused her to catch her breath. Caught, her gaze wanted to linger, but she forced herself to look away quickly. She had the distinct feeling that, had she not, she could well have lost herself.

Not surprisingly then, she was in a state of some agitation as she helped Nick gather up his things. She hid it from him, for the last thing she wanted was for him to worry about her when he should be concentrating on his work. It took barely fifteen minutes, and then he went down to say goodbye to his parents and the other members of his family. Aimi walked outside to wave him off.

She stared after the disappearing tail-lights of his car and, when there was nothing more to see, she made her way back to the kitchen to discover, much to her consternation, that Jonas was the only one there. Standing by the draining board, he was wiping a plate with the ease of a man who had done so many times before.

'Oh!' she exclaimed, totally disconcerted by his presence in what she had thought would be the one place he would rarely venture, and came to an abrupt halt just inside the door. 'Where are the others?'

Jonas shrugged carelessly. 'Outside, I would imagine. I said we'd finish what was left.' He nodded in the direction of the sink whilst continuing to wipe the plate with the tea towel.

Aimi groaned inwardly, for this was exactly the type of situation she had been hoping to avoid. To put it bluntly, Jonas Berkeley was temptation on two legs and, whilst she knew she had the strength to resist most forms of temptation, he was a different matter altogether. Like the siren's song in old mythology, there was something about him which called to her on a totally primitive level. How he made her react without uttering a single word was something she had never experienced to this high degree, and she had thought she knew everything there was to know about herself. To discover she was wrong set butterflies careering around in her stomach.

She groaned to herself, and felt as though she was trapped between the devil and the deep blue sea. The washing-up needed to be finished, and she couldn't just walk away from the task she had started, for then he would know he had her on the run. So she took a steadying breath, walked back to the sink and began to wash a cup. A small silence fell and she felt compelled to break it before it grew into a monster.

'I suppose, in your line of work, you're used to volunteering people for things,' she remarked with heavy irony, and was pleasantly surprised to hear Jonas utter a soft laugh.

'I call it delegating. I pay my staff a good wage to do what I ask,' he informed her, resting his hip against the counter so that he could watch her and still wipe the crockery.

Very much aware of his regard—it was impossible to ignore the way her heart began to thump—Aimi kept her attention fixed firmly on what she was doing. 'They never rebel?'

'On occasion, and I will listen to their opinion, but in the end the decision remains with me. I have a core of loyal people who have been with me for many years.'

'Hmm. You did say you pay well,' she couldn't resist

saying, looking around to see what else had to be washed, and discovering only one last cup.

'That's a very cynical attitude. I prefer to think they enjoy the work.' Having cleared the draining board, Jonas waited for the cup she was washing.

Aimi held it out to him. 'Well, of course you would,' she replied with a wry look. Jonas smiled as he reached for the cup and as he took it his hand touched hers. Already on edge, Aimi gasped, instinctively jerking her hand away, then watched in horror as the fine china cup fell to the floor, shattering on the tiles.

'Oh, my God!' she gasped in distress. 'I'm so sorry!' Without thinking, she squatted and reached for the nearest pieces.

'No! Don't!' Jonas commanded, attempting to prevent her, but it was too late. The glass-like shard had already cut into her finger, causing her to cry out in pain. He muttered sharply, bending down to pull her to her feet. Taking her by the wrist, he held her hand under the cold tap and ran the water. 'I thought you would have known better!'

Wincing as the cold penetrated the cut, Aimi pulled a face. 'I wasn't thinking,' she defended herself, which received a grunt in reply.

'That was patently obvious. Let's have a look.' Turning off the tap, he wiped the cut with a fresh linen napkin he had produced from a drawer. 'Hmm, it looks clean enough. Fortunately, it isn't deep. Here, keep that pressed on the cut whilst I get antiseptic and a plaster.'

Shaken, Aimi didn't protest, but did as she was told. She knew she had been foolish, but her dismay at dropping the cup had been amplified by the way she had reacted to his touch. Stupid, stupid, stupid!

Jonas's return halted her self-castigation and she watched as he bent over her hand and made sure the area was dry before putting on some cream and fixing the plaster. It brought his head closer to hers and in a flash her attention was diverted to the blue-black waves of his hair. She breathed in slowly, the fingers of her undamaged hand itching to run through the dark locks. To know the feel of them.

Lost in her wayward thoughts, she was only vaguely aware of Jonas finishing the task—until, through the sticking-plaster, she was stunned to feel the brush of his lips on the covered wound. She blinked, coming back to the present, only to have her breath taken away when, a moment later, those same lips pressed a burning kiss to the palm of her hand.

'What are you doing?' she gasped faintly, her heart suddenly pounding in her chest.

At the same instant Jonas raised his head, a roguish gleam in his eyes. He did not release her hand; instead, his thumb continued a stroking caress. 'Something I've been tempted to do all weekend. Kiss you,' he declared in a voice as dark and sultry as a passion-filled night.

In the space of a heartbeat, Aimi was struggling. His voice and his touch had her senses spinning out of the stern control she placed over them. She stared at him, almost mesmerised. 'You go too far!' she protested, but there was no power in it.

His lips curved into a knowing smile as his eyes slowly, sensually, quartered her face. 'On the contrary, this is nowhere near far enough, and you know it, darling,' he corrected huskily, causing her nerves to leap wildly.

'Don't presume to know what I'm thinking!' she refuted his claim, even as her ears delighted at the sound of the endearment rolling off his tongue.

Jonas laughed softly, at the same time reaching up to run a finger along the fullness of her bottom lip. 'It's no presumption. I know. We both do. We've known exactly what the other was thinking and feeling from the moment we met.'

Which was the very last thing Aimi needed to hear, for it was true. However, at the same time it was enough to rouse her defences, giving her a breathing space to gather her forces to fight the tremendous urge to give in. 'I know nothing of the sort. I've done nothing to encourage you in this wild fantasy,' she exclaimed, but his laugh was mocking.

'Aimi, you know you don't need to do a thing! We connect on a totally different level.'

Another shockwave swept through her, for the level he was talking about was the one she had sworn would never see the light of day again. Now a sick despair replaced all other feelings and she backed away, drawing her hand from his, thankful he made no move to stop her. 'Well, we're going to get disconnected, because I'm not going to listen to any more of this!'

'Running away won't change a thing. We both know we want each other. It's in every breath we take, every heartbeat.'

Oh, God, she knew just what he meant, and not wanting to feel it didn't make it stop. The sensual pull was stronger than anything she had ever come across, and the desire to explore it a burning ache inside her. She hadn't thought it possible she could want a man with such intensity that she was tempted to forget all the promises she had made to herself after she had lost Lori.

It was the thought of that traumatic time which brought her chin up. 'Maybe it is, but I'm not going to get involved with you, Jonas.' One thing didn't have to lead to another if she remained resolute.

'That sounds good, but we both know you don't mean it,' he came back, taking her breath away.

'Of course I mean it! Why wouldn't I?' she challenged him, and he shook his head, laughing wryly.

'Because this wanting isn't going to go away that easily. It has to burn itself out, and there's only one way to do that. Which is why you and I will have an affair very soon,' he declared with such certainty she could only stare at him speechlessly.

The trouble was, every word he uttered increased her growing sense of inevitability. Yet there was nothing inevitable about it, she rallied instantly. She did not have to follow the path that seemed to stretch out before her, however enticing he made it look. Jonas might be dashing and charming, but she didn't want him in her life. There was no way she could allow him to tempt her into undoing all the good she had done, simply for the fleeting gratification of indulging in a highly sensual affair.

'I wouldn't hold my breath if I were you,' she told him bluntly. 'I'm never going to have an affair with you.'

'Never say never—it's a red rag to any red-blooded male,' he warned her softly.

Aimi tipped her chin defiantly. 'You'll be wasting your time trying to change my mind.'

He smiled sardonically. 'We'll see. I like a challenge. I think you'll prove to be the best one I've ever had.'

That comment sent a wave of anger crashing through her. His arrogance was beyond belief. 'Stay away from me, Jonas.' Aimi followed up that command by spinning on her heel and marching out of the door. Who did he think he was, telling her she would fall into his arms whenever he clicked his fingers? What a nerve!

Fuming, she knew she could not join the rest of the family. Her nerves felt as if they had fire ants crawling all over them and she needed to get away, find some privacy where she could catch her breath and think. Because her defences had just been breached again, and with even less effort than before. She needed to do some repair work—fast.

With that one thought in mind, Aimi took herself off to the library. She didn't bother to switch on the light, but sank down into one of the comfortable leather chairs by the fireplace. Leaning back against the plump squab-bing, Aimi examined the initial source of her present dilemma. Her hand still tingled from the brush of his lips and when she closed her eyes she could feel once again the heat in them as they'd brushed over her flesh.

As she did so, the thought flashed into her mind that, if the internal mayhem she had experienced was the result of a simple kiss, what would something more passionate make her feel?

Half of her knew what the sensible thing to do was, but when he touched her it was her old sensual self who took control. It was an unexpected turn of events, yet, realising where her weakness lay, she knew she had to keep her distance. All she had to do was survive the next couple of days without letting him get close to her and she would be fine. Once she was away from his magnetic influence, the attraction would fade away to nothing. The old Aimi would retreat and the present one would feel more like herself again.

Sighing, she prayed for time to go fast. She needed to get back to the calm she had worked so hard to achieve. Only then would she feel safe.

CHAPTER FOUR

SURPRISINGLY, Aimi slept better that night, probably from sheer exhaustion. She had rejoined the family on the terrace eventually, but Jonas had not been there. Aimi hadn't asked where he was, just breathed a sigh of relief. Now it was morning again, and yet another scorcher.

It being Sunday, the family went to church, but Aimi chose to remain behind. She breakfasted with them but, when they went off to change, she took her notepad and pencils along to the library to continue with her research. Yet, even with the French windows pushed wide, the room felt hot and airless. She persevered for some time, then tossed her pencil aside with a sigh of frustration. It was just too hot.

Thoughts of the cool water of the pool invaded her mind and she wondered if she dare risk it. She figured she had an hour or two before the family returned, and that was plenty of time to take advantage of their absence. It didn't take much more to persuade herself and within minutes she was nipping up to her room to put on her swimming costume under her skirt and blouse. Wrapping sunscreen and a book in a towel, she hurried down again and out through the back door.

Shedding her clothes by a lounger set in the shade of an umbrella, she slipped into the blissfully cool water, closing her eyes the better to experience the pleasure. It was wonderful, and she hummed to herself as she slowly floated across the pool on her back. She lost track of time, so she had no idea how long she had been there when there was a loud splash to her right. Water cascaded over her and she quickly came upright, wiping her eyes as she trod water and looked round to see what had happened.

Down the far end of the pool, a dark head emerged and she knew at once that Jonas had happened. As she watched, he glided to the wall, turned and swam back towards her with a front crawl that produced very little splash. Though she tried not to think it, his power in the water was impressive to watch, seeming to take no effort at all. He stopped when he reached her, grinning at her as he swept his hair out of his eyes.

'Sorry if I disturbed you. I tried not to,' he apologised, eyes twinkling with his particular brand of roguish humour.

It wasn't his swimming that disturbed her, but his presence in the pool. 'I didn't know everyone was back,' she replied, trying to keep her cool and some distance between them.

'Back?' Jonas queried with a raised eyebrow, narrowing that gap with strong movements of his arms and legs.

'From church.' She backed a little further and felt the side of the pool behind her, blocking her retreat. Cursing inwardly at the position she had got herself in, Aimi raised her chin and stared at him.

His smile broadened as he watched her predicament. 'Oh, I never go to church, except on special occasions. Which is why you have the pleasure of my company this morning,' he explained and, as they both trod water, one of his legs just happened to brush against hers.

Aimi knew it was deliberate, but that didn't stop the shockwave which swept through her system. Her lips parted as she drew in a sharp breath, but unfortunately a small wave washed in at the same time and suddenly she was coughing and spluttering.

The next thing she knew, Jonas's arm was round her, his legs tangling with hers as he supported them both with one hand on the pool edge.

'It's OK, I've got you,' he declared reassuringly, though with an edge of humour that was not lost on Aimi.

'You did that on purpose!' she charged as soon as she was able to.

'Would I?' he came back mockingly, and she blinked at him.

It was at this point that she realised she was actually holding on to his shoulders and the tanned skin was so smooth and tactile, her hands were itching to wander. She clamped down on that at once, but then became aware of the strength of his arm around her waist, and that set off a whole new load of fireworks in her nervous system.

'Of course you would!' she shot back pithily, trying to push herself away from him, but he was as immovable as a mountain. She gave up before she made herself look even more ridiculous. 'You can let me go now; I'm fine,' she told him, but he merely smiled.

'That's OK, I'm quite comfortable like this.'

She was sure he was, but she was not. OK, the rebellious part of her that had emerged in the last two days said she could have stayed like this for a long time, but that wasn't the point. The idea was not to be in his arms under any circumstances, putting temptation beyond reach. This was not a good start. Especially as the lower halves of their bodies were entangled like a lover's knot. It conjured up erotic images that did nothing to help her fight her attraction to him but, even as she groaned silently, the means of gaining her freedom came to her.

So, instead of fighting, she smiled at him. 'Jonas,' she said in a sultry voice that the old Aimi had once used to great effect. It made him look into her eyes.

'Yes, Aimi, darling?'

The endearment almost curled her toes, but she resisted it. 'It may have escaped your notice, but my knee is very strategically placed. If I were you, I'd let me go,' she added equally softly, raising her eyebrows to enhance the point.

Jonas let out a soft laugh. 'So it is. Would you do it, though?' he mused, then saw the threat of mayhem in her eyes and relented. 'You win,' he declared, letting her go, and Aimi quickly swam away towards the steps.

Her nerves were skittering as she climbed out of the water, the memory of being held so close to him sending vital messages to her brain, which she did her best to tamp down. She was very much aware of his eyes on her as she walked round to her lounger and towelled herself off. Damn it, now what did she do? She could leave, but that would only convince Jonas he had rattled her. The only thing she could do was stay and bluff it out.

Which was why she gave all her attention to applying the sunscreen, then settled back to read. However, her determination not to look at him was thwarted by the fact she could see him swimming back and forth over the edge of her book. Slowly the book dropped as she watched his powerful form cutting through the water. It was mesmerising, and it was only when he eventually came to a halt that she became aware of what she was doing, bringing the book up again hurriedly.

Minutes later, she caught sight of him out of the corner of her eye. He had left the pool and was heading in her direction. The vision of his lean male body, tanned and glistening with water in the sunlight, closed her throat and dried her mouth. Lord, he looked good enough to eat, she thought helplessly. His black trunks left little to the imagination, and she could feel herself melting in the face of so much maleness. Everything that was feminine in her responded to him, and it was incredibly hard to draw her gaze away before he reached her.

'Good book?' Jonas enquired lazily as he passed by.

'Very,' she replied, though for the life of her she couldn't have said what it was about.

She heard him moving around for a while, then he must have lain down, for she heard him sigh. Peeping round the side of her book, she saw him stretched out on a lounger a few yards away. At least if he was over there, he wouldn't be causing her any problems, she decided, and returned to her book. However, when she realised she had started to read the same page half a dozen times, because she was so busy listening for him, she gave up, closing the book with a snap and tossing it aside.

Sitting up, she adjusted the lounger so she could lie down, then stretched out on her front, resting her head on her arms. Soon the warmth and the quiet made her start to drift off, so it came as a huge shock to suddenly feel hands on her back, gliding up towards her neck. With a gasp she tried to get up, but those same hands urged her back down.

'I'm just putting sunscreen on your back,' Jonas informed her calmly, continuing to smooth his way from her neck to her waist. 'You'll burn in this heat.'

Aimi bit down hard on her lip as his fingers trailed along her ribs, coming dangerously close to her breasts. A bubble of hysteria lodged in her throat, for she was already burning and the sun had nothing to do with it. Lord, she wished he would stop, for his touch was driving her crazy! Jonas, however, seemed intent on taking his time and when he did finally stop she almost groaned. Whether from relief or disappointment it was too close to say.

'There, that should do it,' he declared. 'Unless you want me to do your legs?'

'No!' she refused, a little too quickly. 'I did them myself. Thank you,' she added in a choked voice, keeping her head turned away from him.

'OK. Now you can do my back,' he went on easily, and now she did turn to look up at him.

'What?'

Jonas stared down at her, his expression as innocent as the day was long—only she didn't believe it for a second. 'Do my back for me, would you?' he repeated and, taking her agreement for granted, strode back to his lounger and stretched out on his front.

Sitting up slowly, Aimi reluctantly picked up the sunscreen. A battle began to rage inside her. On the one hand, she knew she should refuse, do the sensible thing, but on the other, the wanton part, which she had controlled for so long, but which had somehow escaped from its icy prison, saw an opportunity to explore the inviting planes of his tanned flesh. It was this part which eventually won the silent argument and, as she crossed the space between them, she ignored the warnings of her reserved self.

Kneeling down beside him, she squeezed the cream into the middle of his back, then took a deep breath and started to smooth it on with her palms. She meant to be quite professional about it, but the instant she touched him there was no way she could remain detached. His skin was firm, yet silken, and the motion of her hands highly erotic. She soon lost track of time, indulging herself in the freedom of the moment.

'Mmm,' Jonas sighed with evident pleasure. 'That feels good. You have wonderful hands. I could get used to this.'

His voice was little more than a sensual growl, but it brought Aimi swiftly back to her senses. What was she doing? she asked herself, horrified. The heat that rose in her cheeks was mercifully hidden by the heat of the day, as she quickly finished the task and sat back on her heels. 'That's it,' she declared, preparing to rise. She needed to get away from him before she did anything else.

Jonas came up on his elbow, catching her wrist before she could move away. 'I haven't thanked you yet,' he growled, pulling her towards him as he spoke.

'Stop it, Jonas,' Aimi protested, fighting to keep her balance, but in the blink of an eye he rolled on to his back and she could only go with him, collapsing on to his chest.

Eyes gleaming with mischief, he slid his free hand around her neck and urged her mouth down to his. Aimi tried to hold herself away, but he was far too strong for her. His lips took hers with stunning sensuality. This was no tentative beginning. It was a lingering kiss that stirred the embers of their mutual passion. His mouth claimed hers, demanding an equal response, which she tried to deny him, but forces stronger than anything she had experienced before decreed otherwise. For aeons she was lost in the heat of his lips and the glide of his tongue. The more she gave, the more she wanted, and it was only the raucous cry of a crow as it flew over that eventually brought her back down to earth with a bump.

Pushing herself away, Aimi stared down into eyes that gleamed with wry humour and something more profound. Her stomach churned with self-loathing that she had once again given in to the selfish pleasures that had once ruled her life. It turned her blood to ice. 'I think you've thanked me quite enough,' she said, rising and moving away from him as she did so. 'Next time just try saying it.'

'That wouldn't be as much fun.' Jonas laughed, watching her pad back to her lounger and lie down on her front, turning her head away from him. 'You enjoyed it, Aimi. Don't pretend you didn't!' he called over to her but she ignored him.

Wincing, she closed her eyes, because the truth was she had enjoyed it. Kissing Jonas had been an incredible experience, and not one she could forget. Over and over, those moments played in her mind. Every sense she possessed had been heightened by the scent, touch and taste of him, just as she had known it would be. The man was an irresistible lure, yet somehow she had to try to resist him, for he was only interested in the fun of the chase. She could not allow herself to be yet another trophy for him.

She had to remember the reasons she had renounced the old Aimi all those years ago. It was so that she could live with herself and what she had done. Unfortunately, the old Aimi had broken bounds and got away from her for a moment, but she would conquer it in the end. She knew it was only a skirmish. There would be harder battles to fight before this was over. She had to be strong, because otherwise how could she live with herself?

Sighing, she willed her body to stop reacting to the male mere yards away. She would not throw herself into Jonas's arms, for he would only use her to amuse himself and she was worth more than that. Much more. This was the main thought in her mind as she finally began to relax, eventually slipping into sleep.

When Aimi awoke a little while later, Jonas had disappeared, and it proved just how ambivalent her emotions now were, that she had to tell herself she was relieved. Gathering up her things, she made her way back up to the house, thankful that the family had not yet returned. A quick shower washed away the signs of her swim, but she wished it were as easy to put the genie back in the bottle. Outwardly she might look calm, but inside she was in turmoil as she thought of the kiss she had shared with Jonas. It made her feel unsettled, and she didn't like it. To combat the feeling, she made sure that her outward appearance was as plain as ever—every single strand of her hair was tied into its pleat and the pins were secured in place. It wasn't the strongest armour, but it was all she had to fight both the inner and outer battle.

She spent the rest of the morning ensconced in the library again, and this time made herself concentrate. Pretty soon she found she had been able to put a pair of dazzling blue eyes out of her mind. She lunched with the family on the terrace, a little surprised that Jonas did not join them, but at least it gave her more time to settle her composure for when he did turn up.

Aimi worked until it was time to go upstairs to wash and change for dinner. As she examined her meagre wardrobe, she had another instance of her ambivalence when she found herself wishing she had something other than skirts and blouses to wear. Immediately her mind's eye saw a picture of Jonas grinning at her, knowing she had changed for him, and her spine stiffened as she fought down the wanton urge. She was not going to fall back into the old ways, when dressing to attract a man had been as normal as breathing. She was a different person. A better person, who was above such things. Which was why, when she climbed out of the shower and dried herself, she put on her royal-blue skirt and her sleeveless white silk blouse.

Her hair smoothed into its pleat and looking cool and efficient, her reflection was a necessary boost for her will-power. The woman in the glass looked as if she could handle anything. But could she? a traitorous voice asked. Aimi had considered herself beyond temptation, but Jonas was proving her wrong. Even now she was still thinking about him, which was a bad mistake, for that brought with it memories of that kiss and the storm it had aroused inside her.

Groaning at her own stupidity, Aimi turned away from her reflection and took some steadying breaths.

You can do this, Aimi. Just remember how hard you've worked to get where you are. Think of Lori, and all you promised her you would do to make up for what happened. Be strong. Be strong.

Some minutes later she was just slipping her feet into her comfortable pumps when there was a rat-a-tat-tat on the door. Surprised, she opened it, only to find Jonas outside. He was wearing a crisp white shirt that brought out the intense colour of his eyes and his hands were in the pockets of smart dark trousers. The effect was definitely easy on the eye and she groaned inwardly. Her senses registered him on levels she had forgotten she even had!

Now he favoured her with one of his trademark wicked smiles. 'As Nick is no longer here, I thought I would escort you down to dinner,' he explained his presence smoothly. 'Are you ready?'

'I think I can find my own way downstairs,' Aimi refused the offer with lashings of irony. However, Jonas was not about to be thwarted.

'I'm sure you can, but my parents did their best to instil a sense of good manners in all of us, so you shouldn't refuse my chivalrous gesture,' he countered, eyes dancing and a grin hovering around his lips.

Realising she was going to look ridiculous standing there arguing with him, Aimi reluctantly stepped outside and closed the bedroom door. 'And there was I, thinking the age of chivalry was dead!' she mocked, heading for the stairs at a brisk pace. Jonas easily fell into step beside her.

'You're a hard woman to please,' he complained, and she laughed sardonically.

'Actually, I'm quite easy to please. If you were to go away, that would please me greatly,' she shot back quickly, and almost jumped when his hand came to rest under her elbow as they descended the stairs. For so light a touch, she felt it to the very depths of her.

'We both know that's not true, darling. I have a pretty good idea what would please you greatly, but leaving isn't it,' he added in a sexy undertone, and Aimi's nerves did a series of somersaults.

It was hard to hang on to her composure when it was under such a strong attack, but she managed. 'Did your parents teach you to be outrageous, too?' she returned smartly, whereupon he laughed huskily.

'No, that was all my own doing.'

He was good at it, too, she thought waspishly. 'Yes, I'm sure it was.'

'You do that very well,' Jonas remarked easily, and Aimi glanced round at him, frowning.

'What?'

'Disapprove,' he enlightened her, and it was her turn to laugh.

'That's because I do disapprove of you,' she insisted firmly.

Jonas brought them to a halt as they reached the bottom of the stairs and turned her to face him. 'Doesn't stop you wanting me though, does it, Aimi?' he challenged, holding her gaze.

To say she didn't want him would be futile, for the man wasn't a fool. He could read women with diabolical ease. 'It will stop me getting involved with you, Jonas.'

He shook his head, supremely confident. 'No, it won't. It will add spice to our affair. I'm looking forward to it.'

Irritated beyond measure, mostly because the resurgent part of her knew he was right, she jabbed an admonitory finger into him. 'Listen to me, Jonas Berkeley…'

His smile would warm a winter day. 'You know, you really are beautiful when you're angry.'

Full of helpless rage, Aimi almost stamped her foot. 'Stop it!'

'I wouldn't, even if I could. I'm smitten with you, Aimi Carteret, and I don't intend to stop until the fever raging inside me dies down.'

As declarations went, it was a show-stopper. It certainly stole Aimi's thunder. She shook her head dazedly. 'What about what I want?'

'That's the beauty of it. We want the same thing, so why don't you simply accept it? I promise you, you won't be sorry.'

Oh, he was golden-tongued and so persuasive—was it any wonder women fell for him in droves? Which was all the spur her pride needed to make sure she didn't do the same.

'You are the most pig-headed man it's ever been my misfortune to meet!'

Jonas started them moving again. 'You won't think so when you know me better.'

'I know you as well as I intend to,' Aimi declared shortly, relieved when they entered the dining room to find the family gathered there. She immediately went to talk to Paula. Her whole body was trembling and her heart was racing. She felt besieged, under constant attack from all sides, totally dismayed by the rapid disintegration of her defences these past few days.

Fortunately, Jonas didn't follow her. Unfortunately,

now that Nick was absent, Jonas had been seated beside
her, so her respite was short-lived. However, he was the
very soul of charm and wit, helping the conversation
flow easily around the table. She had to admire his
ability to put everyone at ease, and knew it was that very
same charm which managed to find a way through a
woman's defences. As she ate the perfectly prepared
food, Aimi had to admit, albeit grudgingly, that there
was a lot to like about Jonas Berkeley—if you ignored
the fact that he was a womaniser and a playboy.

As was the family habit, they had coffee on the
terrace, and conversation turned to this and that. Aimi
asked Simone about her passion for family history and
pretty soon they were lost in the intricacies of Simone's
family. Aimi found it fascinating, so much so that for a
while she quite forgot about Jonas—until he spoke.

'You should show Aimi the family Bible,' he suggested to his mother. 'I'm sure she would be interested.
It's a hundred years old at least.'

'Would you care to see it?' Simone asked her, and
Aimi nodded.

'Certainly. We have nothing like that in our family.'

Simone immediately turned to her son. 'Take Aimi
to the library, Jonas. You know which shelf the Bible
is kept on.'

'I'd be happy to,' he responded with a smile, getting
to his feet and looking enquiringly at Aimi.

This was not quite what she had intended when she'd
accepted the offer, but there was little she could do, so
she rose with every appearance of pleasure and
followed Jonas into the library. Crazy as it seemed, it
felt as if everything was conspiring to bring her and

Jonas together. Even her own pulse had increased its rate in expectation of heaven knew what! Things she wanted, yet didn't want to want. Like the feel of his lips on hers again.

The library was only marginally cooler than the rest of the house, even though it was on the shady side. After ushering Aimi into the room ahead of him, he closed the door, then crossed the room to push open the French windows. The light was beginning to fade, but he switched on a green shaded library lamp which sent out an intimate golden glow.

Aimi watched him from the middle of the room, which had somehow managed to shrink in size so, although Jonas was by the window, it felt as if he were right beside her. Electricity began to hum in the air around them. She could feel it taking her breath away and her awareness of him grew exponentially.

Jonas, meanwhile, had gone to one of the book-shelves Aimi had yet to search and lifted down a large leather-bound tome, which he set on the table near the lamp. Looking up, his eyebrows arched as he saw her some yards away.

'You won't be able to see it from there,' he pointed out, and Aimi finally went to join him. 'Here, you open it,' he invited, allowing her to get to the table in front of him. Of course, once she was there, he closed the gap, his body brushing against hers as he watched over her shoulder.

Aimi did her best to concentrate on the Bible, opening the cover to see that lines of names had been entered there in a fine copperplate hand.

'The third name down is interesting,' Jonas remarked, reaching around her to point to the entry, but Aimi barely saw it, for the brush of his warm breath against her neck sent shivers down her spine. 'Can you read it?'

Read it? She couldn't even remember the alphabet! All she knew was that if she turned her head the smallest fraction, her lips would touch his. 'Not really,' she lied, her voice sounding unreal to her own ears. 'It's very small.'

'There's a magnifying glass around here some- where,' he murmured, looking around. 'Ah, here it is.' He reached over and, as he did so, his cheek brushed hers. Aimi gasped and Jonas went still, turning his head just enough to look into her eyes. 'Is something wrong?' he asked softly, and the gleam in his eyes told her he knew exactly what he was doing and its effect on her.

'No, but I think we should rejoin the others,' she managed to croak out, feeling her lips tingle as he watched her mouth whilst she spoke.

'But you haven't looked at the Bible yet. There's more to see,' he added with sweet persuasion. 'You know you don't really want to leave.'

The old Aimi didn't. The one who had lived life to the full and loved with equal enthusiasm. But the one who knew mistakes had to be paid for still struggled to maintain control. Yet it was taking every ounce of strength she possessed not to turn into his arms and let the heady waters of physical attraction wash over her. Nobody had ever made her feel this need, this urgency. She was being drawn to it like a moth to a flame, knowing she could get seriously burned, yet transfixed by the promise of warmth.

Almost at the point of drowning, Aimi raised a hand to push herself away. 'I have to go,' she declared, knowing she sounded desperate, but not caring right then. 'I have to get some air.' She couldn't breathe in here. He was taking all the oxygen away. With the last of her strength, she moved away and Jonas made to follow her, only to be brought up short by the sudden loud ringing of the telephone. He had to answer it, and that was when Aimi made good her escape.

She disappeared through the French windows as she heard Jonas speak into the telephone receiver. This brought her out on one side of the house, from where she could cut through the shrubbery and head down towards the lake without being observed. She felt like an animal in flight, and her heart pounded with every step she took. Yet, even as she extended the distance between them, she could feel the siren call urging her to go back. What she wanted was behind her, not out here.

However, she knew that not everything she wanted was good for her. She had seen the effect of such self-indulgence, and had vowed it wouldn't happen again. So she headed for the quiet of the wood, hoping to find solace for her restless senses. Only there was no peace to be found, even in the rose-shrouded gazebo tucked away at the far end of the lake, overlooking the water.

Holding on to one of the wooden posts, she closed her eyes as she admitted she was fast losing the battle to resist Jonas. Wanting him was a fire in the blood that could not be quenched. For all her intentions not to get involved, right now the thought of not seeing him again was like a fist tightening on her heart. If that was un-thinkable, then another thing was also true. It had been too late to walk away unscathed from the moment she had first set eyes on him. He had stirred her old self into life again and, no matter how she fought her nature, that self was not about to be denied.

The sound of a footstep broke her thoughts and made her eyes fly open. As if in a dream, she turned towards the entrance. Jonas stood there and it felt to Aimi as if the air around her gave a low, soft sigh. She watched as he stepped inside, instantly shrinking the small building and stealing the sultry air, so she could scarcely breathe.

'You followed me,' she said without surprise.

'You knew I would,' he declared huskily, and he was no longer smiling. 'I'm drawn to be wherever you are. You feel it, too.'

Aimi took a ragged breath. 'Do I?'

Jonas took another step, which brought him inexorably closer. 'It's quite stunning, isn't it, this thing between us? We felt it from the moment we met.'

'Did we?' she challenged, holding up her hand to keep him at bay, but he merely kept on going until her hand was touching his chest. Resting over his heart. There he stopped, and looked down into the depths of her eyes.

'Oh, yes. You know your skin screams to know the touch of mine,' he breathed hotly, and her heart lurched. 'It's the same for me. I cannot walk away from you, Aimi. Not yet. Neither can you run from me.'

'You don't know me that well,' she whispered brokenly, even as her fingers splayed out, feeling the heat coming off him. Without thinking about it, her other hand rose to join its mate, allowing her to feel the strength of his powerful chest and the heart beating beneath it.

'I intend to know you better,' came the soft reply, and she breathed in deeply.

A part of Aimi knew she should make some attempt

to stop him, yet she couldn't. After all the things she had just told herself, the need to know was overwhelming. Her brain shut down, leaving only need to take control. She could feel herself starting to tremble as she looked up at him, and the fire in his eyes held her mesmerised. Then, as his head lowered, it was as if the whole world held its breath. When his mouth met hers, the earth shifted on its axis, never to return to the same spot again.

She felt the touch of his firm lips throughout the whole of her body. It was the most incredible thing. Every sense she possessed came alight in that one instant. Hunger stirred and in a flash the smouldering coals of desire surged to life, sweeping over them, burning them up. There was no way back. Jonas claimed her mouth with a growl of male satisfaction and, with a low groan, Aimi responded, parting her lips to accept the thrust of his tongue. It was wild and hot, one kiss fuelling the next until it was impossible to say where one began and the other ended.

It was pure potent physical attraction and for endless minutes neither could do anything to control it. They were like puppets tossed into a maelstrom of aching need that had surfaced after days of captivity. They had opened the Pandora's box of attraction, drowning in the hidden delights. There were no barriers, no restraints. They were free at last to indulge the needs driving them on.

When the first wild rush of excitement subsided, they drew apart, breathing hard, eyes revealing the power of what they had just experienced.

'Oh, God!' Aimi groaned softly, dropping her forehead until it rested under his chin. 'I had forgotten.' It had been so long since she had allowed herself to feel anything, it was almost like the first time all over again.

'That it could be like this?' Jonas queried thickly, one arm drawing her close to his body, the other hand slipping the pins from her hair until it was a blonde halo that he slid his fingers into to frame her head. 'Heaven help me, so had I.' He sounded surprised—shocked, even.

Aimi was hardly listening. With every breath she could breathe in the scent of him, and the tanned flesh of his neck was temptingly close. All she had to do was turn her head and her lips made contact, sending shivers down her spine. Then her tongue snaked out, flickering over his skin, and her whole sensory system went into overdrive as she heard Jonas catch his breath. But there wasn't enough of him to touch. She wanted more. In an instant her impatient fingers were tugging at the buttons of his shirt until she could push the silk aside and claim her prize.

Not that she had much time to indulge her need to know the taste and feel of him, for Jonas's fingers closed on her hair and urged her head back so that he could see her.

'You're driving me insane,' he declared gutturally, plundering the aching arch of her throat with lips that burned.

Aimi clung on to his shoulders as her body started to turn molten. The strength went out of her legs, but Jonas easily took her weight, easing them down to the floor so that they were kneeling in each other's arms. Then she felt his hands unbuttoning her blouse and pushing it aside, tugging at the silky fabric until it dropped to her waist, revealing the honey-coloured silk of her bra. One long-fingered hand claimed the aching mound of her breast and instinctively she arched her body towards him, her head falling back as she closed her eyes and savoured the scintillating pleasure. His hands moved over her, teasing aside the barrier of silk, blazing a path that his lips followed, until his mouth closed on her engorged nipple, suckling, and she groaned helplessly as her senses went spinning.

By this time there wasn't a sane or sensible thought between them. There was only room for what they could feel and, like pebbles on the beach, they were helpless as each succeeding wave washed over them, drowning them in sensual pleasure. Clothing was tossed aside with fine disregard as they strove to be ever closer and discover each other. They tumbled to the floor, limbs entwined, their passion for each other as hot and sultry as the night around them.

Yet the sheer urgency of the desire which had engulfed them meant that this was to be no long drawn out, lazy lovemaking. They were driven by a purely primal need to reach the goal their bodies craved. Aimi only knew that every erotic kiss, every scorching touch was driving her insane. She longed to feel him inside her. Craved it so that, when Jonas finally slipped between her legs and thrust into her, she cried out at the stunning sensation of being one with him.

Jonas went still. 'Aimi?' he asked in a voice thick with passion. 'Did I hurt you?'

She shook her head swiftly. 'No. I'm fine. It's just…been so long,' she whispered, not wanting to talk right now.

He looked as if he wanted to say more, but she tightened her arms around him, digging her fingers into his back, using his own need against him. He began to move again and within seconds there was no room for anything other than their wild ride towards release. It came like a white-hot explosion, causing both to cry out at the sheer wonder of it. Holding on to each other, they rode the shockwaves of pleasure until even that ended. Then, replete, they slept.

CHAPTER FIVE

A LONG while later Aimi stirred, frowning in confusion as the world slowly made itself felt. Why was her bed hard, and her pillow firm yet warm? As she puzzled over that, an owl hooted almost over her head and finally she realised she wasn't in her bedroom, but outside.

That was enough to have her shooting upright into a sitting position. Stunned, she realised that not only was she naked, but so was the stirring male form beside her. As Jonas slowly opened his eyes, everything came rushing back to her. The moments in the library, followed by their heated lovemaking here in the gazebo.

Her stomach lurched and she felt sick. How could she have let this happen? Dear God, she had spent years distancing herself from the person she used to be, and now, at the drop of a hat, she had tumbled to the floor and allowed Jonas free rein with her body! Just as the old Aimi would, she had let her senses rule the moment. Had gloried in it, in fact, and it was not a comfortable thought.

She hadn't been able to fight her most basic instincts. After all she had gone through, she should have been able to walk away from him, so why hadn't she? Sitting there, in the heated darkness of the gazebo, she was forced to accept what was plain to see. Because she had wanted it to happen. Because she had wanted to feel alive again. To experience the warmth of being with another human being. Yet not just any person, only Jonas.

'Come back. You're miles away.' Jonas's low voice broke into her uneasy introspection.

She turned and looked down at him, seeing the gleam that entered his eyes and the curve of his lips as he smiled. Reaching out a hand, he caressed the curve of her back. She felt that touch in every part of her and her instinct was to lean back against it. She tried not to. Tried to be strong.

'Hmm, your skin is soft, like a peach,' he murmured, coming up on an elbow to test the feel of it with his lips.

Though it was almost like a physical pain to do so, Aimi pulled away. 'Stop,' she ordered, knowing she should leave and go back to the house. Jonas had other ideas.

'Stop?' he challenged with a soft laugh, trailing a line of kisses up to her shoulder, then to the tender skin at the base of her neck.

She knew then just how weak she really was, for helplessly she arched against his touch, unable to summon the strength to leave. Then his free hand framed her face, turning her head so that he could claim her lips in a lingering kiss.

'I don't want this,' she tried again as his lips moved on, her lashes dropping over her eyes as he found the sensitive spot below her ear.

Jonas chuckled throatily. 'I can tell.'

Aimi drew in a sighing breath. 'We can't stay here. You have to stop.'

'I don't think I can,' he whispered as he trailed a line of kisses along her jaw line. 'You'll have to stop me.'

Her eyes opened as he reached her lips again and, as soon as she looked at him, all sensible thought flew from her head. Stopping was the last thing she wanted to do. She placed her hand over his heart, feeling the steady beating under her palm. Ignoring the small voice of caution, she allowed herself to be controlled by her reawakened sensuality. Her lips curved into a smile.

'I've changed my mind.'

With a laughing growl, Jonas sank back to the floor, taking her with him. Neither of them heard the owl hoot from its perch in the tree outside.

An hour later Aimi carefully eased herself out from beneath Jonas's arm and rose to her feet. Gathering up her clothes, she quickly put them on again, then stepped over to the doorway. All was quiet outside, as if nothing monumental had happened in this beautiful place. She turned to look at Jonas's sleeping form and her heart turned over. He looked softer in sleep, his defences down, and just watching him caused a ball of emotion to expand inside her. Making love with him had been the most perfect experience of her life. He was a magnificent lover, but it was more than that. Somehow being with him had made her feel…complete in a way she hadn't felt for a very long time. She had been alive.

And then a memory forced its way to the front of her mind. It was of her best friend, Lori, laughing at her in the sunshine at the top of the ski slope that last winter. They had been eighteen, the world their oyster. They had both known then what it felt like to be alive, but Lori never would again. Aimi's hand tightened into a fist, her nails cutting into her palm. So what gave her the right to feel it now, when a better person couldn't? Because a man had broken through her defences and shown her how incredible sex could be with him? That was not good enough. Nothing would ever be good enough.

What she did now, having crossed the line and given in to temptation, Aimi simply did not know. Which was why she knew she could not linger here any longer. She had some serious thinking to do, and there was no way she could run the risk of Jonas waking up before she had made up her mind about what she was going to do. So, careful not to make too much noise, she hurried down the steps and headed for the path around the lake that would take her back to the house.

Safely in her room, for the first time she locked the door. Without turning on the light, she sank down on to the edge of the bed and dropped her head in her hands. Into her mind came Nick's warning of danger, and she closed her eyes in despair.

'Oh, Nick, look what I've done,' she said out loud, and could picture the look on his face. After all her fine words, she had allowed herself to be seduced by his brother.

What on earth was she going to do? She knew now what it was like to make love with him, and there was no way she could forget it. Lord, how she regretted those moments of weakness. Why Jonas? Why now? Because she had been overthrown by emotions stronger than her sense of guilt. Her desire for Jonas had been too powerful to deny, and she honestly didn't know if she could manufacture defences strong enough to withstand him. She only knew she had to try, because she had given her word to Lori.

Aimi took a sighing breath, pressing a hand over the fluttering nerves in her stomach. There would be no more. She would fight this thing. She could be strong. The mistake didn't have to be compounded, so long as she kept faith with herself. Finally she felt the anxious fluttering in her stomach die down and a sense of calm settled around her.

Her mind made up, Aimi summoned up the energy to shower and slip into her nightie. The heat tonight was even more unbearable than the previous ones, and there was scarcely a breath of air coming in the open windows. Aimi tossed and turned on top of the bed, the heat the least of her problems. Eventually, though, sheer mental and physical fatigue made her fall asleep. However, the dreams she dreamt were as hot and sticky as the night.

Dressing in her ubiquitous skirt and blouse the following morning, Aimi carefully pinned her hair into its pleat. She had to use new pins, getting a flashback of Jonas taking the old ones out of her hair in the gazebo last night. Fortunately she had enough, because she was not going to go back to the scene and retrieve them. Her memories were vivid enough without that!

Once she could look herself in the eye in the mirror without wincing, Aimi was ready to face the day. She descended to the ground floor, where all was still silent, it still being early. The housekeeper must have been busy, though, for the windows and doors were already open. Aimi stepped out on to the terrace, her spirits buoyed by the sight and sound of the birds searching for their breakfast. Leaning against the low wall, she watched their antics for quite a while before suddenly the hairs on the back of her neck stood up, alerting her to the fact she was no longer alone.

She half turned, knowing exactly who she would see. Her radar was specifically designed to pick up on one man. Jonas stood in the doorway, his expression thoughtful as he observed her. Their eyes met briefly and she could feel his trying to probe hers, trying to see beyond the contained front she exuded. When he failed he walked towards her and she turned back to the view, not wishing him to get even the smallest hint of how her heart turned over at the sheer pleasure of seeing him. 'Hey, what happened to you last night?' he asked as he slipped his arms around her waist. Automatically her hands came up to try and remove them, but he resisted her efforts with ease. 'I missed you,' he growled as he pressed a kiss to the spot where her pulse fluttered like a trapped bird.

Aimi felt the touch throughout her whole system, and fought the urge to let his strong body take her weight. 'I was tired so I went to bed,' she responded coolly. That was better. Cool was good.

Jonas turned her around, and she could see the deep frown between his eyes. 'What's wrong?'

Her eyebrows rose. 'Wrong? What could possibly be wrong?' she charged with a dash of mockery.

'You tell me,' he returned, still frowning. 'Last night you were all heat and passion. This morning you're…'

'Back to normal?' she put in for him, adding a faint laugh for good measure. 'What did you expect?'

He stepped back a fraction. 'Not this.'

Somehow Aimi managed to look amused, but it was by no means easy. 'Was I supposed to be all over you like a rash because you managed to break down my resistance?'

Jonas clearly didn't like her tone. 'Actually, I thought you would welcome the idea of spending the day together.'

Aimi shrugged, determined to put on a show of indifference that would keep him at bay. 'I can't help what you thought, but I'm here to work. Besides, what more could you possibly want? You had me. Now you can add me to your list.'

It could have been her imagination, but for a moment she thought Jonas actually looked taken aback. It vanished beneath a heavy frown. 'What the hell are you talking about?'

Once again she shrugged, as if it was all too much bother, whereas actually her nerves were jumping about like crazy. She was not enjoying this at all, yet she had to press on. 'Look, you saw me, you wanted me, you had me,' she spelled it out for him. 'End of story.'

His eyebrows rose at the blunt way she had said it. 'It's far from being the end, Aimi. What about the little fact that it had been a long time between lovers for you? You should have told me,' he charged her, and Aimi felt the colour flood into her cheeks.

Put on the defensive, she folded her arms so he couldn't see her hands tremble. 'And when would I have done that?'

A muscle flexed in Jonas's jaw, then he sighed and dragged a hand through his hair. 'I take your point. I just wish I had known.'

Aimi shifted from foot to foot, wishing he would drop the subject. 'What difference would it have made?'

A faint smile curved the edges of his mouth, and there was a faint twinkle in his eye. 'I would have acted differently. Been more gentle.'

That remark, plus the look in his eye, deepened her colour again. 'You were gentle,' she assured him, quite unable to lie about that. 'You didn't hurt me.'

'Really? I thought I must have done, after your cold reaction this morning.'

'You mean that's never happened before?' she asked sceptically, and his smile was rueful.

'Once or twice. I just never expected it from you.'

Her chin came up. 'Why? Because I made it so easy for you?' she couldn't help snapping back at him, and he frowned yet again.

'Is that what you think? That you were easy?' Jonas asked in surprise and she looked away, her jaw working madly, feeling as if the situation was getting away from her.

'It doesn't matter. Last night was a mistake,' she declared flatly, for the truth was she knew she had made it easy for him by forgetting the principle by which she now lived her life.

'Do you regret what happened?' he challenged immediately, and just a little sharply, which surprised her.

She cast him a quick glance before concentrating on the view of the garden. 'It shouldn't have happened. It wouldn't have done if…' Aimi caught herself up swiftly, but Jonas latched on to the words.

'What would have stopped it, Aimi?'

Aimi was still smarting from her own self-castigation and his question roused her anger. She spun round, jabbing a finger at her chest. 'I should have stopped it. It isn't as if I didn't know better! I just wanted…but that was wrong. I know that now.'

Jonas shook his head, clearly bemused by the way

she was behaving. 'What's going on in that head of yours?' he queried, taking her by the shoulders. 'All we did was make love.'

Aimi shrugged him off. 'We didn't make love; we had sex.'

Jonas took a step back, something dark flickering in his eyes. 'If I just wanted sex, there are any number of places I could go,' he declared tautly.

Aimi had the strangest feeling that she had hurt him, and yet she couldn't think how. Besides, she couldn't allow herself to weaken. She had already said far too much. 'Then I suggest you go there next time. I won't be available.'

Jonas stared at her in silence. 'You don't think very highly of me, do you?'

She drew in a ragged breath, knowing the truth was she didn't think very highly of herself right now. 'Your reputation speaks for itself.'

He laughed bitterly. 'Does it, indeed? Would it interest you to know that I'm not quite the love 'em and leave 'em bastard the press insists on painting me as?'

'It doesn't matter. Whatever you think there is between us, I'm ending it right now,' she declared firmly. There, she couldn't have made herself any clearer.

'Why? Scared you might enjoy it too much? And, before you open those delicious lips and hit me with a bunch of lies, you did enjoy last night. I have the scratches on my back to prove it!'

That stopped her in her tracks and she stared at him, absolutely mortified. 'You're lying,' she gasped, shaking her head in swift denial.

Quick as a flash, Jonas had pulled his shirt from his

trousers and turned, raising the back to show her the red welts. 'Does that look like a lie?' he demanded, swinging to face her again and tucking his shirt back in. 'You were a tigress, sweetheart. And I know that all I would have to do is take you in my arms and kiss you, and you would get that love-drugged look back in your eyes. It wasn't just sex. We made love, whether you care to call it that or not.'

His words were a pointed reminder of what she had been trying to forget. Uttering a strangled sob, she bit her lip and looked away. 'So help me, Jonas, if you don't shut up, I'll scream!'

'Do it,' he taunted softly. 'I like the way you scream.'

'Damn you!' Pushed to the end of her tether, Aimi swung round, hand raised to strike him. Jonas stopped her easily, catching both wrists and securing them behind her back, an action which brought her body up against his. Chest heaving, she stared up at him.

'That's better. Now you remind me of the woman I know. There's fire in your eyes and heat in your blood. That's the true Aimi Carteret, not the woman with ice in her veins you want to project!' he declared with grim satisfaction.

Aimi paled, feeling sick as she realised she had fallen for his tricks and displayed yet again the side of herself she had tried to keep locked up. Steadying the raft became imperative, and she called on all her experience in order to restore calm. 'Let me go, please,' she commanded in a more reserved tone and, when he complied, she moved away from him. 'Thank you,' she added, still with the same cool control, and Jonas shook his head.

'You should have been an actress, with that command over your emotions,' he remarked ironically, and Aimi laughed.

'I discovered a long time ago that I had no real talent for it,' she corrected him, seeing again her mother's wry acceptance that her young daughter would not follow in her footsteps.

'You were wrong. You have an amazing ability to cover what you're really feeling. It's an act I suspect you've honed to perfection over the years.'

Aimi shot him a frosty look. 'This is not an act. This is who I am.' She had not pretended to change herself; she had actually done it!

He smiled faintly. 'It's who you would like to be. I've seen the other you, and I like her better.'

'Because she slept with you?' Aimi retorted with a curl of her lip. 'Well, she won't be doing it again.' Now she knew the old Aimi could resurface at any time, she would be taking more care.

His smile broadened. 'Don't be so sure of that. I can be very persuasive. I'm not ready to say goodbye yet, Aimi. Last night has only made me want more.'

'That's too bad, because last night made me realise I had had more than enough!'

Jonas laughed and it was whilst Aimi was battling the urge to slap him, because he wasn't taking her seriously, that Paula emerged from the house.

'Goodness me, you two are up early!' she exclaimed with her customary jaunty good humour. 'Lord, what a night! I feel like a wrung out dish rag!'

'It was hot,' Aimi agreed, inordinately grateful for the change of subject. Moving along the wall, she put more distance between herself and Jonas.

'Very hot,' he agreed, and the glint in his eye told Aimi the heatwave he was talking about had nothing to do with mother nature.

'What time were you thinking of driving back, Jonas? We're going early, trying to beat the crowds,' his sister interrogated him as she flopped into a chair at the table.

'After lunch. Aimi probably needs to spend a few more hours in the library, doing Nick's research,' Jonas responded, quirking a questioning eyebrow at her.

Now that Paula was here, Aimi found it easier to keep her composure. 'I do have some work to finish up,' she confirmed.

'You can always come back any time to do more. Mum and Dad would be glad to see you,' Paula said, smiling warmly at Aimi. 'Listen, I've been thinking. We all live in town, so why don't we get together for dinner one evening? Me and James, Nick, Jonas and you. Wouldn't that be great?' She beamed from one to the other, seeking support.

Right then, Aimi couldn't think of anything less great. 'I'm not family, Paula. You shouldn't include me.'

Paula swiftly knocked that idea on the head. 'Nonsense! I know we haven't known each other long, but I like you, Aimi. Please say you'll come,' she urged, her eyes as huge and wistful as a spaniel's.

Aimi knew when she had been backed into a corner, and gave the only answer she could under the circumstances. 'All right, I'll come,' she agreed, knowing she could always beg off at the last minute, and Paula clapped her hands.

'Marvellous! I'll do all the arranging, so you just wait for my call.' Having arranged matters to her satisfaction, Paula immediately jumped up and went in search of her other half to tell him the news.

Jonas pulled a wry face. 'Paula is something of a runaway train at times, but she means well.'

She looked at him for the first time since his sister had joined them. 'I can see that. I like Paula, but I doubt very much if I will be free that night.'

'Running away won't change anything,' Jonas remarked sardonically, and she didn't pretend not to know what he was talking about. 'This isn't over, Aimi.'

'It is if I say so. And there's no need to trouble yourself about giving me a lift. I'll take the train,' Aimi added for good measure.

'You won't,' Jonas corrected at once. 'Unless you're prepared to tell my parents why you don't want to go with me. You're stuck with me, so get used to the idea,' he enlarged with a mocking smile. 'Look, if anyone wants me, tell them I've gone for a run around the lake. Unless you want to join me?' he invited.

Aimi shook her head quickly, still smarting over the fact that she couldn't refuse to go with Jonas without causing a fuss. 'You go. I have work to do.'

'Think of me while I'm gone,' Jonas said with a laugh, then turned and trotted down the steps to the lawn. Moments later he was jogging over the grass.

Aimi watched him go, unable to stop herself admiring his rear view. He was, without doubt, a near perfect specimen of manhood, but he was not for her. It ended here. The sooner she was safely back in the real world, in her own life, the better. Then she would forget all about Jonas Berkeley and those heated hours down by the lake.

* * *

The remainder of the morning Aimi spent with her nose buried in books, but there was no avoiding having lunch with the family. Naturally, Jonas was there, but he kept his distance from her and never gave even the slightest hint that his interest in her was more than casual.

In fact, he paid so little attention to her that she began to hope that he might have had a change of heart—until she caught him looking at her, and the heat in his gaze was enough to burn her up on the spot. Her reaction was beyond her control. She gasped faintly, heat rising into her cheeks, and there was a taunting twist to his lips as he glanced away again. The same thing happened once or twice more during the course of the meal, and she realised that he was being deliberately provocative in a situation where she could do nothing to stop him. All she could do was grit her teeth and bear it.

In the early afternoon, Aimi packed her things ready for the return journey. She was not looking forward to it, but she had faced worse situations. Calling on all her powers of self-control, she carried her bag downstairs to take her leave of the family for the last time. Whilst Jonas stowed her case in the boot of his car, she said goodbye to his parents, who had been so welcoming and made her short stay so enjoyable. Then it was time to be off.

It was a roomy car and Aimi was able to make herself comfortable without brushing shoulders with him. She had brought her notebook with her and, as soon as they were under way, she flipped it open and gave it all her attention. Her intended aim was to keep busy the whole journey, but she glanced up in surprise when, after they had gone less than half a mile, Jonas suddenly steered the car off the road into a lay-by.

'Is something wrong?' she queried automatically, watching him unfasten his seatbelt.

'No. I've merely forgotten something,' he responded blandly, and she frowned.

'Is it important?'

'Absolutely,' he confirmed, moving towards her. 'I've forgotten exactly how those luscious lips of yours taste,' he added, slipping a hand around her neck before she knew what he was about, and pulling her towards him.

Too late, she realised she had been neatly tricked by a master. Though she raised a hand to hold him off, her seatbelt held her trapped as his lips found hers, taking them in a powerful kiss. Aimi tried not to respond, but her wilful senses rebelled. They would not obey her silent command and in an instant she was floundering, her lips parting to allow him to plunder her mouth in a deeply satisfying way that sent *frissons* of pleasure winging through her entire system. She was quivering when he eased away to look down at her and the wicked glint of triumph in his eyes made her bite her lip and look away.

'Ah, now I remember!' he exclaimed softly, running a finger over her lower lip until she had to draw in a ragged breath.

She looked at him then, eyes dark with anger directed as much at herself as to him. 'Damn you!' The words were a croak, and ultimately telling.

'Stop fighting it, Aimi. You know you don't want to.'

'I do! Leave me alone!'

'I couldn't even if I wished to. I want you too damned much,' he replied, brushing her lip with his finger once more, before righting himself, locking on his seatbelt and setting the car in motion again.

Aimi turned her gaze to the window, but she saw very little of the passing countryside. Her thoughts were a mess. Why couldn't she be stronger? Why was it that every time he touched her, she simply melted? Why didn't she have the backbone needed to keep her word to her friend? *I'm so sorry, Lori.*

She sighed wistfully, closing her eyes, unaware that the small sound caused Jonas to look round with a frown. Maybe it was a trick of the light, but he saw a vulnerability in the curve of her cheek that gave him pause. There was more to Aimi Carteret than met the eye, and he realised he wanted to unravel the mystery of her. Without quite knowing why, he knew it was important. Not one to question his instincts, he switched on some soothing background music and sat back to mull over just how he would do it.

Unaware of all this, and bone-weary from all the emotional ups and downs of the past few days, Aimi's thoughts began to drift. Before she even realised it, she was asleep.

When she eventually awoke, the music was still playing softly but, instead of being upright in her seat, she was angled to one side, her head resting on Jonas's shoulder. Aimi knew she ought to move, but couldn't quite bring herself to do so right away. Being close to him like this meant every breath she took brought with it the scent of him and, though she knew it was a mistake, she couldn't help indulging herself for a moment. There was the subtle fragrance of his cologne and, beneath it, another that was the pure male scent she recalled so very vividly from last night.

They took a bend and she was fascinated by the way Jonas's hands moved on the steering-wheel. They were long-fingered, capable, and it didn't take much effort to recall them moving over her body, arousing her to a fever-pitch of need. The sensual thought sent heat racing through her veins, increasing her heartbeat and short-ening her breath in a flash.

Finally alarm bells went off in her head, reminding her that she was flirting with danger through her indul-gent thoughts. She was supposed to be dampening down her desire for the man, not stoking the flames! It was the spur she needed to move and she sat up abruptly, putting as much space between them as she could.

Jonas took his eyes off the road long enough to glance at her quizzically. 'Bad dream?' he asked as he returned his gaze to the road ahead.

She almost laughed, for the whole situation between them was like a bad dream. 'You shouldn't have let me fall asleep on you. You should have given me a nudge,' she returned, hoping he hadn't guessed what had been going through her mind.

'You looked too comfortable,' Jonas observed with a shrug of the shoulders.

She had been comfortable—very! 'I never would have done it had I known,' she explained, needing to make sure he knew she hadn't changed her mind.

'I know, which is why I left you,' he said lightly, then flashed her a rakish grin. 'I was indulging myself. I liked having you so close to me,' he confessed flirtatiously.

'Well, I hope you made the most of it, it's the last

time it will happen,' she told him firmly, only to hear amusement in his voice when he answered.

'So you keep telling me. Who are you trying to convince—me or yourself?'

Aimi didn't answer, for the truth was she supposed she was trying to convince both of them. Everything was going wrong. Part of her didn't want to want him, whilst the other wanted to revel in it. To experience everything. To know some joy for however long it lasted. She did know that the more she was with him, the harder it was going to be to walk away. Yet that wanton side kept asking why she had to walk away at all. Her conscience told her why she should but, as more time went by, she didn't know if she could. Last night, everything had seemed so simple, yet it was anything but.

She looked at him, wondering just what it was that made him so different from all the other men she had met. Why was it she couldn't seem to say no and mean it when it meant so very much to her to do that very thing?

'Figured it out yet?' Jonas asked, without taking his eyes from the road.

She jumped, having been lost in her thoughts. 'What do you mean?'

'Whether it's safe to go with your instincts or not.'

'That would rather depend on which instinct you're talking about,' she answered with a wry touch of humour. She had two, and they were pulling her in opposite directions. Right now, she didn't know which would win, and that was something she wasn't used to. Her path had been so clear, but now it was like looking through frosted glass.

'You're too intelligent to make the wrong decision,'

he informed her lightly, and she pulled a face he couldn't see.

'I don't think intelligence has anything to do with it,' she replied dryly.

'There's nothing wrong in wanting someone, Aimi. It's the most natural thing in the world. Take a risk. What's the worst that can happen?'

A chill ran through her as his words brought back the memory of Lori on the last fateful day they had been together and the full horror of what she was fighting against. Lori had said pretty much the same thing. Taking risks had been part of their lives then, and she had found out the hard way that the worst that could happen was that somebody died.

The skiing holiday had started out so well, too. They had planned it for months. Lori Ashurst had been her best friend since boarding school. They had spent holidays together every year. Their families were wealthy and had indulged their offspring, so that both girls had learned to ride horses, scuba-dive and ski, amongst other things. They had been taking a gap year, having worked hard to get places at university. Young and oblivious to everything but what they wanted, they had partied hard and done outrageous things, and generally had a good time. Neither had known that the good times were soon to come to an end.

It had been Aimi's idea to ski off-piste, and Lori had agreed it was a great idea. They had known it was risky, but taking risks was the only way to go—then. So they had set off, and it had been great fun. They had whooped with the thrill of it as they'd traversed the slopes…and then it had happened. An overhang had fallen off higher up the mountain, setting in motion a devastating avalanche. Both of them had felt its advance at the same time and had stopped to look behind. They had been right in its path, and fear had galvanised them into action. Signalling Lori to head to the side, Aimi had set off, expecting her friend to follow her, but Lori had decided to go another way. It hadn't been until Aimi had reached the relative safety of the trees that she had dared to stop and look back. She had been horrified to realise Lori wasn't behind her, and then terrified when she'd seen her friend still in danger. She had cried out, but the thunder of the crashing snow had taken her voice away. Then it was too late. She had seen the avalanche swallow Lori up. For one moment she had caught sight of her crashing downhill and then she had gone from sight. Gone for ever.

The avalanche of guilt which had crashed down on Aimi then had been every bit as devastating as the one that had killed her best friend. Another skier had seen what had happened and had called for help, but it had been too late for Lori. The experienced rescue team had found her body after hours of searching, and seeing her taken away on a stretcher had underlined for Aimi that it was she, and not the avalanche, that had really killed her friend. It had been her idea that they should do it, and she had known that Lori always followed where she led. If she hadn't wanted to experience the thrill of off-piste skiing, Lori would still have been alive. It had been her fault. All her fault.

Drowning in a sea of guilt, Aimi had remembered all the times Lori had tried to persuade her not to do things, but she would not be swayed. She had ignored Lori's fears and gone on selfishly to do whatever it was, and now Lori was dead and there had been nowhere else to look for blame than to herself.

Aimi had accompanied her friend's body back to England and during that awful plane journey she had sworn to change. To turn herself into somebody that people could admire. Someone who was a responsible member of society, and who could be relied upon. There would be no more shopping and partying. No more meaningless romances with handsome young men. She would be the antithesis of the old Aimi in every way, for how could she let herself have fun when Lori could not?

Guilt was a terrible thing to live with, and the most awful thing was that Lori's death had been put down to misadventure. At the inquest she had been confronted by Lori's parents. They, too, blamed Aimi, and the things her mother had said in her grief only added to Aimi's burden. She had barely been able to bring herself to face them at the funeral, and they had simply ignored her. Aimi's mother had tried to console her, telling her it had been an accident, but Aimi had known it wasn't true. It had been her fault and she had to atone for it. It was the only way she could live with herself.

To her mother's alarm and horror, she had cut herself off from her old life completely. Had thrown herself into her studies, then into her work, and over time had slowly come to find a kind of peace with herself. She had learned to laugh again, to take some pleasure from the world around her, but she had never been able to forgive herself. Because of that, she could not allow herself to have the things that Lori would never have.

Nothing had happened to alter the course of her

life—until she had met Jonas. He had made her feel things she had thought she never would again. He had invited her to re-enter the world she had sworn to forsake, because it was the one she had inhabited with Lori. The dilemma Aimi faced was that she wanted to go there but, if she did, she would be betraying her friend. How could she do that?

It ought to have been easy to say no, and last night she had been determined to turn her back on it, but with every second that passed, and despite everything she said, she could feel her resolve weakening. Would it hurt, just once, a small voice asked, to drop her guard and allow herself to know some joy again? Would it be so very wrong? Dared she, as Jonas wanted, take the risk?

CHAPTER SIX

IT WAS several hours before Jonas finally drew the car up before the apartment block in which Aimi lived. Holiday traffic had clogged the roads, turning a simple journey into a nightmare. Aimi felt like a limp rag, for the temperature in the city was higher than the countryside. She knew her apartment was going to feel like an oven, and wasn't looking forward to entering it after the better part of four days.

All through the remaining part of the journey she had been plagued by her memories, reliving that awful time over and over again in her mind. For some years she had been haunted by nightmares, but that had slowly faded, so that she rarely had one now. It wouldn't surprise her, though, if she had one tonight.

When Jonas switched off the engine the sudden silence was deafening. She still did not know what she was going to do. She knew that she ought to walk away, and yet no sooner had the thought entered her head than a voice cried out inside her, *No, I'm not ready to give this up! I don't want to be put back in the cold and the dark yet! I want to live! I want to have this!*

Staggered by the strength of the feeling, Aimi felt dazed, but at the same time she knew she had just been given her answer. The resurgent Aimi had won, drowning out the small voice of her conscience. She simply could not walk away from this right now. She had tried, but it was just too strong to fight. As soon as she accepted that, her inner battle came to an end. Like magic, she could sense the restraints which had held her back falling away, and deep inside it felt as if a small bird had woken from a long sleep and was flapping its wings as it prepared to fly free.

Almost light-headed, she turned to Jonas with a cool smile that hid a certain amount of inner turmoil. Even though she knew the path she was going to take, she felt nervous. She knew she was stepping out on a limb that was far from secure. It wouldn't take much to knock it down. 'Thank you for bringing me home. It must have been out of your way,' she said politely.

One eyebrow rose at her tone, and his lips twitched momentarily. 'I gave Nick my word that I would get you home safely,' he returned ironically and, because her anxiety level was heightened, that answer stung.

'Yes, well, you've done that,' she responded, gathering up the notes she had barely looked at for hours and slipping them into her bag. 'I'll be sure to tell him you did a marvellous job.' She couldn't stop herself giving him the pithy reply because it dawned on her that she didn't know how to tell him she had changed her mind.

Fortunately it bounced off Jonas the way everything else she had ever said had done. 'OK, let's get you inside,' he declared, opening the door and climbing out.

Aimi scrambled out, too, whilst Jonas retrieved her

case from the boot. 'There's no need for you to come all the way upstairs,' she told him, feeling edgy and not a little ridiculous as she headed for the door to the building in his wake.

'Trust me, Aimi. Need is the reason there is every need,' he retorted dryly, and her heart took a sudden wild lurch. 'I've just spent a tortuous number of hours locked in a car with you, unable to so much as lay a finger on you for fear of having an accident!'

Her senses reacted wildly as she heard those words, and her pulse took up a faster rhythm as she looked at him. 'Did you want to touch me?' The provocative question slipped out before she even knew she was going to say it. Once said, though, she knew it was the perfect solution to her dilemma, so she held her breath for his answer.

When he looked round, the fire in his eyes was enough to singe her. 'What do you think?'

Jonas studied her carefully for a moment, as if he had at last seen the subtle change that had taken place in her. He took a deep breath and laughed wryly. 'It's a wonder I'm not insane!' He held the door open for her to precede him inside the building.

The lift was on the ground floor, so they stepped in and Jonas pressed the button for her floor. Leaning against the back wall, Aimi looked at him, wondering at the sea change this man had wrought in her in so short a space of time. Such was the power of him that for the moment her demons were totally vanquished.

Jonas couldn't have made it any clearer that he wanted to kiss her, and she wished the lift would go faster. Desire was a flickering ember deep inside her, and it was growing stronger with every passing second.

His head turned, blue eyes blazing hot. 'If you keep looking at me like that, we'll never make it to your apartment,' he growled seductively, and she shivered in anticipation.

'I don't think we should rush into this. Maybe you should see me to the door, and then go,' she said, suddenly feeling slightly nervous.

His laugh was taut with emotion. 'Don't freeze up on me, Aimi.'

Her eyes were huge as she looked at him. 'You want me that much?'

'I've never wanted a woman more. Does that surprise you? Why? You're a beautiful, intelligent, extremely sensual woman.'

It was instinctive for Aimi to shake her head. 'I'm not,' she denied, and he laughed.

'Don't argue with me or I might just have to come over there and prove it to you. Which would be highly dangerous; I only have so much control left.'

Her nerves leapt as their gazes clashed and became locked in a heated exchange that pulsed in the air between them. By the time the lift door opened, Aimi was finding it hard to breathe and her legs barely had the power to carry her. She didn't care what was wrong or right any more—all she knew was she wasn't going to think about it now, she would think about it tomorrow. She fumbled for her key in her bag as they approached her front door and Jonas took it from her, unlocking the door with impatient movements. Then they were inside with the door shut, and he turned to her, almost tossing her case aside.

Aimi dropped her bag to the floor just as Jonas took

her into his arms and kissed her with a searing depth of passion. She was swept up in it, returning each kiss only to discover that their mutual hunger increased, becoming ever more powerful. Her hands went around his neck, needing to explore the strong male shape of him, but only came in contact with his shirt. It had to go, and her hands fumbled to push it from his shoulders. Realising what she was doing, Jonas took his arms from around her and helped her to undo the buttons and push the shirt down his arms, then he urged her back against the wall, holding her there with the weight of his body as he pulled her blouse from her skirt and slipped his hands under it, exploring the silken skin beneath.

Aimi lost her breath and dragged her mouth from his, whereupon Jonas swiftly dealt with the buttons of her blouse and tugged it off her arms, tossing it aside as he pressed his lips to the valley between her breasts. She could feel her body responding, her nipples tightening into aching points that yearned to be touched by the lips mere inches away. At the same time she longed to explore the firm male body pressed so intimately close to hers. Her fumbling fingers tugged his shirt free of his trousers, and then she could experience the heady pleasure of running her palms over the undulating planes of his back.

Nothing could describe the delight she felt when Jonas arched into her touch, and she caught the low moan of pleasure he gave. Then it was her turn to gasp as his hands glided up her spine, released the catch of her bra and pushed it upwards, releasing the swollen globes to the mercy of his seeking lips. When he took her engorged flesh into his mouth, she thought she would die, then his tongue flickered over one tight nub and she cried out with the intense pleasure of it.

Of course, that was not enough for either of them, and in short order shoes, skirt and bra were all tossed aside in passionate abandon. In the next instant Jonas had lifted her up and settled her on his hips, pressing her back against the wall as his lips and tongue once more plundered her breasts. Aimi folded her legs around him, hands tangling in the dark silk of his hair, neck arching back as she savoured the pleasure he was administering.

When he raised his head and looked up at her, she could see the need in his eyes despite the gloom of the unlit hallway. 'Where's your bedroom?' he asked in a voice made gravelly by passion.

'The first door,' she could only gasp back as her heart thundered inside her.

Pushing them away from the wall, Jonas carried her down the hall and into her bedroom. In three strides he was at the foot of the bed, knelt on it and lowered them both on to the covers. Swiftly, the remainder of their clothes were discarded by impatient fingers and finally they were free to explore each other without any barriers.

Jonas came up on one elbow and explored the velvety slopes of her body with eyes and hands, and it was highly erotic to Aimi to watch him concentrate on learning the shape and feel of her. His touch was so gentle it was almost reverent, and aroused her to a pitch of need she had never experienced before. Because of it, she was not afraid to let him see what he was making her feel, arching her body into his touch, uttering helpless little sighs and moans as he stoked the flames of her desire with sensual mastery. When, eventually, his lips followed the path laid down by his hand, seeking out the hidden core of her femininity and laving it with exquisite strokes of his tongue, she closed her eyes and let herself drown in the sea of pleasure.

Yet she was not inclined to take a passive role for long. She had to give as well as receive, and when his ministrations threatened to plunge her over the edge of reason, she took control by trailing her nails down the sensitive skin of his spine, making him catch his breath and straighten up. With her body still pulsing from the pitch of desire he had aroused, she set about working her own magic on him. To her infinite delight, he was as sensitive to her touch as she had been to his. His flat male nipples responded as hers had to the brush of her tongue and the nip of her teeth, and when she heard him gasp in pleasure it brought a cat-like smile to her lips.

She wanted him to feel what she had, and used all her ingenuity to arouse him. His body was perfect—firm to her touch yet as smooth as hot silk. She explored every inch of him and he abandoned himself to whatever she cared to do. Slowly, and with infinite care, she trailed her hands and lips down his body, over his taut flat stomach until her fingers found and closed around his hard male shaft. Jonas's whole body jerked as his breath hissed in sharply between his teeth. He muttered something that sounded like a prayer and Aimi glanced up, fascinated to see the man she thought of as unflappable gritting his teeth in a superhuman effort to retain control.

She took pity on him, taking pleasure instead in exploring her way back up his body until she could look down into his eyes. Jonas brought his hands up and framed her face, his thumbs brushing across her lips.

'You have the ability to drive a man mad,' he murmured scratchily.

'That's only fair, because you're driving me insane, too,' she whispered back.

At that he rolled them over until he was resting over her, his hips cradled on hers. 'I have a cure, but if I use it there will be no going back. If you want me to stop, this is your last chance.'

Aimi had no intention of asking him to stop, so she smiled a sultry smile and moved against him. 'You're talking too much. Don't you know actions speak louder than words?'

Jonas caught his breath as her movements sent a wave of heat rushing through his veins. 'OK, OK, I get the message,' he responded with a growl, and stopped talking to start some interesting moves of his own.

From that point on the only sounds were their sighs and moans of pleasure. It was hard to know where one body ended and the other began as tanned limbs tangled in a timelessly sensual dance that stoked the already incandescent fires of need. When Jonas finally entered her, Aimi experienced a moment of intense joy that had nothing to do with passion. Nothing in her life had ever been so right as this moment of joining with him. She felt complete in a way she had never known before and knew that without him she would never again feel whole.

The moment was lost when he began to move, his thrusts controlled to give the maximum amount of pleasure to them both. Yet that very pleasure fed on itself, creating a need for more that was a tight coil inside her. Every move she made to meet and deepen his thrusts increased the tension, and when she heard

Jonas groan achingly she knew he had lost the power to control his actions. There was only their mutual driving towards a goal that seemed just beyond their reach. Then Jonas gave one final desperate thrust which pushed them both over the edge in a white-hot climax that had them both crying out.

Aimi held on as they floated through a kaleidoscopic world of the most intense pleasure. It seemed an age before they came back down to earth, and the reality of the two of them wrapped around each other on her bed. With a sigh, Jonas moved on to his back, taking her with him so that she was tucked into his side, her head resting over his heart.

'What did I tell you? Extremely sensual,' he murmured into her hair, and Aimi gave a barely audible sigh.

Tonight with Jonas had felt like discovering herself all over again. Yet it wasn't the same as before, because Jonas had made it different. It was totally new, totally incredible. She wanted to savour it, because she knew it couldn't last. Eventually Jonas would start to drift away, as he always had, and she would have to let him go. But not yet. Not yet.

Aimi was roused before dawn next morning by the soft brush of lips on hers. Blinking to focus her eyes, she smiled groggily when she saw it was Jonas leaning over her.

'Good morning,' she greeted gruffly, still full of sleep, running her eyes over the face and body of the man she had spent last night making incredible love with. A frown darkened her brow as she noted the clothes he was wearing. 'You're dressed.' Her heart sank, though she didn't know why.

Jonas smiled regretfully. 'I know. It's early still, but I have to get back to my place to get ready for work. I have several important meetings today. I made you some tea.' He picked up the mug he had set on her bedside table.

Aimi wriggled into a sitting position and took the mug from him. 'Why didn't you just go? You could have left me a note,' she pointed out, taking a sip of the hot liquid.

'Because that way I wouldn't be able to kiss you goodbye, now would I?' he explained simply, and Aimi stared at him solemnly, whilst inside a long-buried imp of mischief rose to the surface.

'You don't have to. I know what to expect,' she declared with a sigh of resignation, then fought down a smile as Jonas immediately frowned back at her.

'Just what is it exactly that you expect, Aimi?'

She shrugged diffidently, whilst acknowledging that he was remarkably easy to tease. 'That you'll pretty much come and go as you please, for as long as it suits you. When you find someone else, you'll be gone. Don't worry, I'm not going to make a fuss,' she assured him resignedly, taking another sip of tea. To her amusement, he looked quite grim.

'Let me get this straight. You think I'll turn up for a quick roll in the hay, then be off about my business again? A wham-bam-thank-you-ma'am kind of thing?'

His tone was so steely, she knew he was really taking her seriously. Which was why she decided to string him along for just a little longer. 'What else?'

After looking at her long and hard for several minutes, making her think for a moment that he had seen through her ruse, Jonas took the mug from her and set it down on the bedside table again. 'And just where did you get that idea?'

Aimi bit down hard on her lip, lest she start to giggle. 'That's how it is with men like you, isn't it?' she managed to challenge in a small voice, and his reaction was anything but small.

He snorted in disgust. 'No, that isn't how it is with me. You have a lot to learn about me, Aimi Carteret, and we'll start with this. I do not want every woman I meet. Those I am attracted to, it is for more than sex. I want to know her. I want to enjoy her company. I like giving her presents and making her happy. Sex is just a part of it, not the whole.'

She blinked at him, taken by surprise. 'Oh!'

Now he smiled again, that roguish twist of the lips that made her feel warm inside. 'Is that all you can say? You were eloquent enough a moment ago?' he taunted softly, and she realised she had, indeed, been found out.

'You knew,' she accused, and he laughed.

'Not right away, but then I remembered just what a good actress you are.'

'You're not such a bad actor yourself,' she shot back, for he had fooled her.

'It wouldn't do my business any good if everyone could read what I was thinking,' he informed her dryly. 'I had no idea you could be a tease. Is it any wonder I find you endlessly fascinating? I've never met anyone like you, and that intrigues me.'

Aimi made herself comfortable against the pillows and smiled winsomely. 'Really? Tell me more.'

'What would you like to hear? That I know there's a warm, lovely woman under the cool exterior you adopt, and I want to see more of her?' he charged in a soft voice that shivered over her nerve-endings like a warm summer breeze.

Her throat closed over, making her voice husky when she responded. 'You've seen pretty much all of me already.'

Jonas's smile faded whilst the heat in his eyes grew. 'I have, and it takes my breath away. I'm glad you changed your mind and decided to take a chance on me.'

A tiny voice tried to make itself heard, but she forced it back down. 'So am I.'

He studied her for a moment in silence, then uttered a heartfelt sigh. 'Damn, but you're beautiful. Do you take after your mother? Is she beautiful, too?'

Aimi smiled fondly as a picture of her mother formed in her mind. 'I think she's the most beautiful woman in the world. I have her eyes.'

'Just her eyes?'

'Uh-huh. And I've heard people say I have my father's chin,' she added, touching the gentle cleft there.

'Heard?' Jonas queried, one eyebrow raised.

She shrugged fatalistically. 'He died when I was small. I never knew him.'

'That's a shame. I'm sure he would have loved you.'

Surprise shot through her at such a statement coming from him. 'How can you know that?'

Jonas grinned and tapped the tip of her nose with a finger. 'Because fathers always dote on their daughters. It's a prerequisite for the job.'

All of a sudden Aimi could feel tears burning the back of her eyes at the notion that the man she had never met would have loved her just because she existed. 'I'd like to think that's true,' she admitted huskily, and Jonas frowned as he noted the way her eyes glittered like diamonds.

'I didn't mean to make you cry,' he apologised gruffly, and Aimi gave him a watery smile.

'They're happy tears. I'm feeling a bit emotional today. Thank you for saying what you did.'

'You're welcome,' he replied, and bent forward to press a soft kiss to her lips. 'Now I really must go.'

With his departure imminent, Aimi found herself wanting to throw her arms around him and keep him there. She didn't, though she was tempted. Neither did she ask the other burning question: when will I see you again? 'Don't work too hard,' she advised instead.

'I'll try not to,' he promised, leaning across to kiss her deeply, and when he broke away she could see the banked fires in his eyes. 'That will have to see me through the day, unless you're free for lunch?'

Aimi shook her head regretfully. 'I won't have time. I'm working on a draft of a lecture your brother is due to give.'

Jonas was amused. 'So I have to make way for my brother, do I? Ah, well, at least I won't have to worry about who might be flirting with you. Nick never thinks of anything but work,' he said brightly.

With that he rose, pressed another swift kiss to her lips and left the bedroom. Moments later, she heard the front door open then close behind him. Immediately, Aimi sank back against the pillows and hugged herself. She looked back over the last few days and the amazing changes that had happened. It was almost too much to take in, yet she wouldn't change a thing. She had made her bed and was content to lie in it.

With a sigh she slipped down beneath the single sheet, intent on getting a few more hours sleep. She wasn't going to worry about the future or what might happen. Better to live in the now and enjoy these moments whilst she could.

Aimi was late that morning, for the first time since she had started to work for Nick. She had quite forgotten to set her alarm and consequently had overslept. As she let herself into his house, she felt oddly unsettled for having had to rush.

'Sorry I'm late,' she apologised breathlessly when she entered the study to find Nick already writing at his desk. He looked up at her, did a double take, then his jaw dropped. Aimi blinked back at him in surprise. 'What is it? What's wrong?'

Gathering himself, Nick waved a hand in her general direction. 'Your hair,' he said simply, and she raised a hand to it, shocked to find it hanging down around her face.

'Oh, my goodness! I forgot!' she exclaimed, feeling oddly vulnerable. Sitting down at her desk, she pulled a container of pins from a drawer and quickly pinned her hair up in its pleat with fingers that actually shook. How on earth could she have forgotten? It was one of the first things she did every day—putting on her armour against the world. Except this morning she had been thinking about Jonas, and fixing her hair had quite slipped her mind. 'There!' she exclaimed with a final pat to make sure all was secure.

'How do you do that without looking?' he asked in some awe, and Aimi laughed.

'Practice. How did the operation go?' Sliding her

chair forward, she picked up the large desk diary that ordered his daily workload.

'It was touch and go for a while, but I think we're over the hump now. I had to wait in case we needed to go back into surgery, but that didn't happen.'

Aimi looked up with a relieved smile. 'Oh, that is good news. At least we won't have to bump anything today.' Very quickly she ran over his timetable with him. There were one or two things to swap around, but the rest was fine.

Nick sat back in his seat and watched her as she turned on her computer and quickly typed in the new information. 'So tell me, did Jonas behave himself when he brought you home yesterday?'

The unexpected question made her nerves leap out of her skin, and she felt warmth enter her cheeks. 'Of course he did,' she confirmed swiftly. 'What made you ask?'

'Because you're not acting like you this morning,' he observed, and she very nearly groaned, for she knew that already.

'It's this heat,' she explained without making eye contact, praying he would drop the subject. 'It's making us all out of sorts. It's got to break soon.'

'Amen to that,' Nick responded, diverted, and the subject was soon forgotten.

They worked together in harmony for the next hour, then Nick left to go upstairs and get ready for his first appointment at the hospital. No sooner had he gone through the door than the telephone on her desk rang demandingly.

Caught in the middle of rephrasing a particularly knotty paragraph, she picked up the receiver with a sigh. 'Berkeley residence, Aimi Carteret speaking,' she responded in her usual fashion, then felt the hairs on the back of her neck rise just as the caller spoke.

'Hello, Aimi Carteret.'

A thrill travelled the length and breadth of her body as she recognised the voice, even though she had known who it would be in that split-second of silence. Her heart seemed to skip a million beats and her senses leapt to attention.

'Jonas?' Her voice sounded low and breathless to her own ears, as if she hadn't used it in an age.

'Were you expecting someone else?' Jonas asked, his tone low and mellifluous, sending a shiver down her spine.

Stunned all over again by her reaction to him, she leaned back in her chair and spun it so she was facing the window and the garden beyond. 'I wasn't expecting you to call. Is something wrong?'

'Nothing's wrong—unless you count my state of mind. I'm actually in the middle of an important business meeting,' he revealed wryly.

That made her frown. 'Oh, I don't think so. I don't think anything would stop you doing business.'

He laughed. 'Up until five minutes ago I would have agreed with you.'

Aimi felt a smile start to curve her lips. 'So what happened five minutes ago?'

'I suddenly experienced an urgent desire to hear the sound of your voice.' The confession stole her breath away, and her heart seemed to expand in her chest.

'What?' Aimi could barely get the word out.

This time when he laughed, there was the strangest edge to it. 'I know. Who would have thought it, but I love the way you talk to me in that sharp way when you're irritated, and in that soft breathless tone you have when we make love.'

If she hadn't been sitting down, her legs would never have held her up. 'You're crazy!' It had been a long time since she had had this kind of telephone conversation with a man, and she had forgotten how much fun it could be.

Jonas chuckled. 'The men in the other room probably think so. I don't usually walk out in the middle of a discussion.'

'But you did, just to talk to me?' Aimi felt a deep sense of warmth invade her system, filling her from top to toe. It even felt as if her heart swelled a little. Another heavy sigh came down the line.

'The need to hear your voice was stronger than my desire to buy the damn business we were discussing. I thought it would help to ring you, but I think it's backfired.'

Aimi closed her eyes and bit her lip. 'Backfired?'

'Now I want to see you, and touch you, too,' he admitted with a sexy growl that swept its way through her body like wildfire, setting her nerves tingling and her blood pulsing thickly through her veins.

Whatever her voice was doing to him, his was a sensual caress to her ears. 'Stop! Don't do this!' she commanded, but there was no real conviction in her voice.

'What am I doing, Aimi?' The urgency in his voice tightened the muscles in her stomach. 'Is it anything like what you are doing to me? Is your pulse racing and the blood zinging through your veins?'

'Jonas, I have work to do! How am I supposed to concentrate?'

'Tell Nick you're not well, and take the day off. I'll do the same.'

Her eyebrows rose. 'Can I be hearing correctly? You're suggesting missing out on a business deal just to see me? It could cost you millions!'

'Aimi, darling, you would be worth every penny!'

'I bet you say that to all your women!' she taunted, whilst experiencing two different emotions. She liked to think what he said was true and hated the sound of all these nameless, faceless women.

A short silence followed before he answered. 'On the contrary, you're the first.'

Aimi didn't quite know what to say, or how to feel. 'If that's true, then I'm flattered,' she responded simply. 'Unfortunately, I can't take your advice because I have work to do, and you need to help this company that is in trouble. You do that, and I'll make you dinner tonight.'

'And if I can't save it?' he questioned wryly.

'Then I'm sure you will have done your best.'

'So I still get dinner?'

'Of course.'

'You have a deal. Now I'd better go before they think I've changed my mind. I'll be looking forward to tonight.'

'Goodbye, Jonas,' she said with a sigh, and heard the phone go down at his end.

She was smiling as she spun her chair round and returned the receiver to its rest. It had been such a long time since she'd enjoyed a flirtatious conversation over the phone. But then, she hadn't wanted to flirt with anyone until Jonas had come into her life. He had changed so many things in the last few days, and they were still changing. Where it would all end? She had no idea, and wasn't about to think about it.

Humming softly to herself, Aimi turned to her computer and did her best to concentrate on her work, despite the fact that Jonas's wicked smile constantly invaded her thoughts for a long, long while.

CHAPTER SEVEN

BY THE time Aimi arrived home that evening, she was excited yet nervous. It was so long since she had cooked for anyone but herself, and she had no idea what Jonas liked. Deciding it was still too hot to eat anything heavy, she planned to make a vegetable risotto, to be served with a fine wine and fresh bread.

It wasn't a difficult meal to make, which was just as well given her state of nervous anticipation. She prepared all the ingredients in advance, which gave her ample time to take a leisurely bath and wash her hair. Then, after drying her hair and slipping into burgundy silk underwear, she went to examine her wardrobe.

It was, to put it mildly, less than inspiring. She didn't even possess a posh frock.

Her work clothes were all functional, designed to tell everyone she was serious about what she did, and her casual clothes were too casual for dinner. She ought to have gone shopping, but it was too late now. In the end she chose a pair of lightweight grey trousers and topped them with a sleeveless cream silk blouse.

Looking at herself in the mirror, for the first time in

a long time, she regretted that she had nothing more feminine to wear. Oh, her lingerie was silky and sensual, but nobody was ever meant to see it. However, there was nothing she could do now, so she sighed and put her hair up again. She could have left it loose, but it was hard to let go of all her old habits at once. One day, perhaps, but not now.

Returning to the living room, Aimi carefully set the table with her best linen and china. She liked fine things, and the crystal glasses she took from the cabinet were truly elegant pieces of craftsmanship. When she was satisfied with how it looked, she went back to the kitchen, put on an apron to protect her clothes and started preparing the cheesecake she planned to have for dessert.

When the front doorbell rang some fifteen minutes later she glanced at her watch, surprised to see it was only a quarter past seven. Too early for Jonas, she imagined it was her neighbour, Ruth, who was always running out of milk or sugar. Wiping her hands on a tea towel, she went to answer the summons and was startled to discover it was Jonas after all.

'You're early!' she exclaimed stupidly, and he pulled a wry face.

'I know. I waited as long as I could, but the need to see you got the better of me, so here I am,' he confessed with a boyish grin.

Aimi got that bubbly feeling inside again, and couldn't help but smile back. 'So you are. You'd better come in.' She stepped back as he entered, shutting the door behind him, and was about to turn when he took her by the shoulders and drew her towards him.

Pulling her into his arms, he lowered his mouth to hers

and kissed her with long slow, deliberation. Aimi melted against him with a sigh of pleasure, knowing she had starved for this all day. When Jonas raised his head again, she looked up at him mistily and he smiled down at her.

'When you look at me like that, all I want to do is pick you up and carry you off,' he confessed huskily.

'But you can't. I'm cooking dinner,' she pointed out just a little breathlessly, and he uttered a resigned sigh.

'I guess I'll have to wait, then. But there is one thing...' Before she could stop him, Jonas neatly whipped the pins from her hair, letting it fall freely about her shoulders. 'There, that's better. Now you look like the woman who fell asleep in my arms last night.'

Aimi's smile slipped a little. She hadn't been prepared for him to do that, and her nerves jolted. Half shorn of her image, she felt more than a little uncomfortable. Yet the way he was looking at her stilled her automatic move to restore order. 'It will get in the way,' she protested half-heartedly as he ran a smoothing hand over the silky blonde mass.

'But you'll leave it anyway?'

'Yes,' she agreed, knowing that to do otherwise would make him wonder what all the fuss was about. He probably thought it was just something she did for work, but it was more than that. She might have taken a giant step in order to have him, but there were still many things she could not talk about.

He grinned roguishly. 'Then lead me to the kitchen and I'll help you with dinner.'

'Can you cook?' she asked over her shoulder, leading the way.

'We'll soon find out.'

As it turned out, Jonas was quite comfortable in the kitchen and clearly cooked for himself when the mood took him. Taking off his jacket, he hung it over the back of a chair and rolled up his sleeves. Amused, Aimi gave him some tasks to do, and they chatted whilst she whipped up the cheesecake and set it in the dish.

The domestic atmosphere was enlightening to Aimi and the same companionable mood spread into the living room when they carried their meal through and sat down to eat it in the slight breeze from the window beside them. Aimi couldn't remember ever being so relaxed and, as the evening wore on, her guard lowered until it was virtually non-existent. She felt almost... euphoric, as if she had been released from an immense burden. She knew she was happy, and it was a good feeling.

Jonas insisted on making the coffee and when he returned with it she looked up, smiling, tossing her hair back as she did so. He went still in the act of setting her cup down, and her smile turned to a frown as she watched him.

'Do that again,' he directed, which only puzzled her more.

'Do what again?'

'Toss your hair back like you just did,' he enlarged, and her frown deepened.

'Why?'

'Because it reminded me of someone, and I can't place her,' he mused. He studied her frozen features for a moment or two, then shook his head. 'No. It's not coming. Has anyone told you before that you look like someone else?'

Aimi's heart sank and she got a sick feeling in her stomach. If she told him she looked like her mother, then there was every chance he might recall the stories that had been spread across the world's newspapers about the famous actress's daughter. She did not want that. Did not want him probing her past. Did not want him to know what kind of person she had been. She had to steer him away from the dangerous rocks.

'No,' she denied as evenly as she could. 'Nobody has. I don't think I'm the kind of woman who looks like anybody else,' she added with an uneasy laugh.

Unaware of the turmoil he had unleashed inside her, Jonas smiled as he finally sat down. 'They say we all have a double somewhere in the world.'

'I think one of me is quite enough,' she responded with an atavistic shiver.

'Have you always worn you hair up?' Jonas asked next, and Aimi groaned as he refused to let the subject drop.

'When I was younger, I used to leave it down,' she admitted, trying to be casual when memories were surfacing that made her uncomfortable. Yet she realised that if she made her answers too secretive, he would start to wonder why. She had to tell the truth, so far as it went. 'I...began to pin it up when I went to university.'

'I would have thought that was the time you would start letting your hair down!' Jonas teased gently and, though Aimi smiled, those same memories made her feel cold inside. She had already let her hair down far too much by then.

Sighing, she shrugged. 'You'd think so, but I was serious about my studies. I...needed to work hard. The last thing I wanted was distractions.' Only by burying herself in work had she been able to survive.

Jonas rested his chin on his hand and watched the play of emotions cross her face. 'You mean male distractions. I can see why you would get a lot of interest.'

Aimi winced, picking up her spoon to idly stir her cup of coffee. 'Yes, well, I wasn't interested. I just wanted to work.' To forget—only that had never been possible.

'So you started putting your hair up,' he mused, only to frown faintly. 'From my point of view, that wouldn't work. You had your hair up when I met you, and I wasn't deterred,' he reminded her with a grin, and she had to smile.

'I wore glasses, too.'

His brows rose. 'Do you need them?'

Aimi shook her head. 'No, but it's true what they say. Men don't make passes at women in glasses.' They had stayed away, and she had been free to go about her studies.

'You could have had fun, too,' Jonas remarked softly, and she looked at him sharply.

'I told you—I was there to work. Besides, I had made someone a promise, and I wasn't about to forget it,' she added solemnly. Then, because she could feel the weight of that promise still, she made an effort to raise her spirits. 'Blondes have a bad time of it, you know. If we're not thought of as dumb…'

'Then it's as some kind of sex object,' Jonas filled in the blank for her. 'I can understand your position. Beautiful women sometimes have a hard time being taken seriously.'

There was no way Aimi could agree with his placing her in that category. 'I'm not beautiful.' Once, with the vanity of youth, she might have thought so, but that Aimi was long gone.

Jonas, however, was not about to be gainsaid. 'You are to me, even with your hair tied back.'

Aimi smiled, as she was supposed to do, yet shook her head. 'Maybe I don't want to be seen as beautiful.'

He laughed softly. 'Beauty is in the eye of the beholder. I took one look at you, and you reached parts of me I had forgotten about. You could wear a sack and my response would be the same.'

She sighed as his words touched her heart. He was a good man, in a world where good men were hard to find. No matter what, she could never regret knowing him. 'You don't have to say things like that. I'm content to be here,' she told him simply. A choice, once made, had to be lived with, whatever the eventual outcome. Yet she knew she dared not look at this moment too closely, for fear of what she might see.

Jonas reached across the table and took her hand. 'I'm just telling you the truth, Aimi. There's no ulterior motive.' Turning her hand over, he rubbed his thumb over her palm. 'Except, perhaps, to reassure you that you can trust me.'

Her brow furrowed. 'Trust you? I do trust you.' Why else would she be here?

Sighing, he enfolded her hand in both of his and looked at her steadily. 'I'm trying to say you can trust me with your demons, too.'

Her nerves crashed against each other in sudden alarm. 'My demons?' The question stuttered out of her suddenly dry mouth. Oh, Lord, what was he implying? What did he know? 'W-why do you say that?'

'Because you were muttering and crying in your sleep last night,' he informed her, and her throat closed over.

'Th-that's ridiculous!' she denied faintly, yet knowing it was possible. She had woken up crying many times in the past. She had been afraid the bad dreams might resume. Now it seemed her worst fears had been realised.

Jonas raised his eyebrows questioningly, resisting her attempts to pull her hand free. 'Is it? It didn't seem ridiculous when I soothed you until you quietened and fell back asleep.'

Aimi stared at him, not knowing he had done that for her. 'I'm sorry if I disturbed you,' she apologised diffidently, and Jonas sat forward.

'You didn't disturb me. I was concerned for you. You sounded desperately unhappy.' The sound of her quiet sobbing had chilled his heart. 'I know how painful inner demons can be.'

The confession took her by surprise. 'You?'

'Me,' he concurred with a wry smile. 'I once gave a man my word that I would save the factory that was his pride and joy. I thought I could do it, but unfortunately things turned bad and I couldn't keep my word. That gave me bad dreams for a very long time, but eventually I beat the demons by doing better for others.'

She stared into his eyes for a moment, then dropped her gaze to their joined hands, for his words had struck a chord with her. 'Some demons are harder to fight than others. Some acts can never be forgiven,' she declared quietly. Caught on the raw, she was speaking from the heart.

'True. But some things are not for us to forgive. That is for a higher authority. Do you want to talk about it?'

he asked softly, and she looked up quickly, only then realising she had said far too much.

'There's nothing to talk about,' she denied with a
swift shake of her head, managing to free her hand at last.

'Aimi…' Jonas began, only to stop when she shot
him a fierce look.

'Don't!' she commanded with authority. 'I get bad
dreams from time to time. They're nothing for you to
worry about. Please leave it alone.' He looked as if he
wanted to argue but, after a moment's thought, shrugged
fatalistically.

'Very well,' he agreed calmly. 'Just remember, if
there is anything you want to talk about, I'll be here.'

Aimi took a steadying breath, very much aware that
she had almost lost her vaunted calm. Though she hadn't
really revealed anything, Jonas would have to be quite
dense not to realise she had secrets. She would have to
be more careful in future.

'Thank you for the offer, but I doubt that I shall need
it.'

'It stands, anyway,' Jonas countered, then adroitly
changed the subject.

The conversation became more general after that,
and Aimi was slowly able to relax again whilst she
listened to him talking about his meeting with wicked
humour. However, even that couldn't stop her yawning
as tiredness slowly settled over her.

'Sorry,' she apologised the third time, and Jonas
laughed ruefully.

'I'd better be off, so you can get to bed,' he declared
as he stood up.

Aimi stared at him in surprise as she got up, too.

'You're leaving?' she queried, completely astounded. She had assumed he would want to stay the night.

Jonas read the look on her face with ease. 'I know what you were thinking, but I came to be with you and share a meal. It was never my intention to leap into bed with you. Don't get me wrong. There's no place else I would rather be, but I wanted to prove to you that this relationship is not just about sex.'

Aimi couldn't stop her heart doing a crazy flip-flop in her chest. 'What is it about?'

Jonas pulled her unresisting form into his arms and kissed her deeply. When he raised his head, she could see the banked fire in his eyes. 'This is about you and me getting to know each other. I already know what makes your body respond to mine and mine to yours. Now I want to know what makes you tick.'

'Why?'

'The why comes later,' he said, releasing her. 'Now, see me to the door,' he urged, holding out his hand, which she took and they walked to the door, where he held her by the shoulders and stared down at her broodingly. 'Thanks for the dinner. It was delicious.'

Bemused, Aimi smiled up at him. 'Are you sure I can't tempt you to stay?'

Jonas closed his eyes with a groan. 'Darling, you could tempt me to do anything, but I promised myself I would do this. Goodnight, Aimi. I'll call you tomorrow.'

Aimi watched him walk past the lift to the door to the stairs. He paused briefly to glance back and raise a hand, then he vanished through the door and was gone. Shutting her front door, she leant back against it, pondering the unexpected turn of events.

She had had a terrible shock when Jonas had told her about the way she had cried in her sleep. It had been a tense time, and she was amazed that he had let the subject go. She knew he only wanted to help, but she could not talk about what had happened in the past because she wasn't going to think about it. Couldn't allow herself to, if she wanted to cling on to the happiness she had.

Thinking of Jonas reminded her that this was not how she had envisioned the evening turning out, but at the same time she was undeniably pleased. She wasn't exactly sure why it should be important, she just knew it was. It was as if he understood her better than she understood herself.

She shivered and pushed herself upright with a brisk shake of her head. Determinedly she walked back into the living room and set about clearing the table. She did possess a dishwasher, but found there was something quite satisfying in cleaning up a meal she had prepared and cooked, so the crocks went into the bowl and she hummed to herself as she carefully washed and wiped.

It was getting late by the time she had finished, and she took herself off to her lonely bed. Changing into her nightdress, she lay down and pulled the spare pillow into her arms, hugging it tight. Closing her eyes, she hoped the nightmares would stay away and her dreams would all be of Jonas.

Next morning, Aimi made sure her hair was securely pinned before she left for work. Nick was operating today and would already be at the hospital, so Aimi let herself into his house and ensconced herself at her desk, determined to get through a small mountain of paperwork.

However, no sooner had she started than her thoughts drifted to Jonas. Last night he had been different, and she really didn't know what to make of it. Pushing her chair back, she rose to her feet and crossed to the window, staring out at the immaculately well-kept garden.

He was a mystery—far from being the Lothario she had once thought him. He had managed to soothe her night fears without her even knowing he was doing it. Why had he done that? And, having done it, why had he stuck around? A lot of men would not have been interested in…what did Jonas call them…her demons. Yet he had wanted to help if he could. It was as strange as his comment that he wanted to get to know her better. Why would he want to do that, and why did it make her feel warm inside to know that he felt that way?

Sighing, Aimi abandoned her introspection and went back to her desk, knowing she had more questions than answers and not enough time to think them through. She had barely settled in her seat, though, when the front doorbell rang. She listened, heard Nick's housekeeper go to answer it, and was studying the pages she was going to transcribe when there was a quick knock on the door and the housekeeper walked in.

'This just came for you, Aimi,' she declared with a bright smile, holding out a long narrow box to Aimi, who took it with a look of surprise.

'For me?'

The other woman laughed. 'It has your name on it,' she insisted and went out again, closing the door softly behind her.

Aimi had a good idea what was in the box, so she was smiling when she lifted the lid. Lying in a bed of pure white tissue paper sat a single deep pink rosebud. It was perfect, and all of a sudden she felt moisture enter her eyes. Reaching inside, she lifted the rose and breathed in deeply, her senses instantly flooded with a heady, creamy scent. Only then did she notice the card which was tucked in at one side.

Her heart missed a beat when she read the simple message, written in a strong male hand: *I missed being with you, Jonas.*

Aimi's throat closed over, for she had missed him, too. The rose made her feel better, though, and she went off to the kitchen in search of a vase to put it in. Then she set it on her desk where the warm breeze wafted the scent over to her. For some reason she found it much easier to settle down to work after that, and was concentrating hard some fifteen minutes later when the telephone rang.

'Did you miss me?' Jonas asked in a lazy tone when she took the call.

As ever, the sound of his voice set her nerves tingling expectantly. 'Yes,' she replied honestly. 'Thank you for the rose. It's beautiful.'

'The florist said it was called Amy, so I knew it was the one for you.'

She smiled to herself at his words. 'The scent is heavenly.'

'As are you,' Jonas returned smoothly.

Aimi shook her head, even though he couldn't see her. 'You don't have to shower me with compliments, you know.'

'I know,' he confirmed, 'but I happen to like doing it. I don't think you've had enough of them lately.'

She frowned. 'What makes you say that?'

'Because it makes you uncomfortable to receive one. However, I intend to change all that by lavishing compliments on you left, right and centre,' he told her teasingly.

'Don't be silly!' Aimi protested, feeling rather odd inside. 'I haven't done anything.'

Jonas's voice became low and intimate, 'Darling, you exist, and you're beautiful. You have a fine mind and a good heart, all of which are worth complimenting. They are also worthy of…' He broke off for a split second, before adding, '…more than that.'

Aimi had no idea what he had meant to say, only that he had stopped himself at the last minute. Not that she minded, for what he had said was more than enough for a spirit that had been bruised for many years.

'So, is that why you rang, to pay me compliments?' she asked and could sense him smiling.

'Partly. The other was to tell you I've booked a table for dinner tonight. Hold on a moment.' The line went quiet for a few seconds, then Jonas came back. 'Sorry about that, but I have an important call on the other line. I'll pick you up at seven, if that's OK with you?'

'It's fine,' she assured him. 'Take your call. Bye, Jonas.' He rang off, and she put the receiver down again, her thoughts in a whirl.

It would, she realised, be very easy to fall in love with a man like Jonas, but she wasn't going to do that. She was far too sensible to mistake a powerful sexual attraction for love. Having come this far, admittedly further than she had ever intended, she was going to enjoy what they had for as long as it lasted.

For the first time in a very long time, Aimi skipped

lunch to go shopping. She could not go to dinner in one of her working suits, however smart they were. Fortunately there were some good shops nearby and she easily found what she wanted. In fact, the choice was so hard to make that she bought a small selection of items and carried them back to the house with a sense of excitement and a floaty feeling in her stomach.

Midway through the afternoon, Nick returned from the hospital and the first thing he noticed when he walked into the study was the rose sitting in its vase on her desk.

'You have an admirer, I see,' he remarked teasingly.

Aimi felt her cheeks grow pink as she glanced from the rose to her employer. Nick had been quite clear that he didn't want her to get involved with his brother, which left her in an awkward situation. 'It's nothing,' she demurred, hoping he would move on, but Nick was clearly intrigued.

'Who is he? Anyone I know?'

The heat in Aimi's cheeks doubled in strength, and she found she couldn't look him in the eye for more than a second or two. 'Oh, no!' she refuted hastily. 'I…um…don't think so.'

The smile vanished from Nick's face as he studied her scarlet one. 'Oh, no, Aimi, you didn't fall for Jonas's line!' he exclaimed in disbelief. 'It is him, isn't it? After all I said!' He paced away from her, then turned back abruptly. 'I could see it coming. I saw him looking at you, but I thought you had more sense. I could kill him!'

Aimi rose to her feet, her heart thumping madly at seeing him so upset by what he thought his brother had done. 'I'm a big girl, Nick. Jonas did nothing that I didn't want him to. It was my choice.'

He looked at her, dragging a hand through his hair in a helpless gesture. 'Don't you see, Aimi? He's very good at making a woman think it's all her own idea. My God, I thought that with you at least he would keep his hands to himself! When I see him, I'll…'

'Do nothing,' Aimi declared firmly, and that brought him to a halt. 'Thank you for worrying about me, Nick, but this really has nothing to do with you. Getting involved with Jonas was my choice, and I'm happy with it. Please don't be angry with him.'

Nick heaved a huge sigh. 'I just don't want to see you hurt.'

She smiled reassuringly. 'I won't be. My eyes are wide open.'

He didn't look happy, but he had to follow her wishes. 'All right. As you say, it's your business. Just be careful. Promise me that.'

Aimi nodded, relieved that he had calmed down. 'I will be, and I'm sorry if I've disappointed you.'

Immediately Nick looked contrite. 'You haven't. I'm just over-protective where you're concerned. It's a big wide world out there, and it's not always a safe place.'

She wondered what he would think if he knew just how much of the big wide world she had already experienced. She knew just how unsafe it was, but with Jonas it wasn't the same. For all that their relationship would be a fleeting one, he made her feel quite safe and secure.

It was a strange feeling for her to have, given Jonas's reputation, yet she trusted him instinctively. When she had time, she would have to ponder just why that should be.

CHAPTER EIGHT

THE next few weeks were a magical time for Aimi, who didn't allow herself to question what she was doing but simply lived for the moment. Whenever her conscience attempted to raise its head above the parapet, she forced it back down again, not wanting to listen. Yet, even whilst she enjoyed the blossoming relationship, she couldn't throw off a feeling that she was living in a house of cards that would soon come crashing down around her.

She had imagined Jonas would want to dine out every night, and be seen in all the smart places, but discovered the opposite was actually true. Sometimes they did dine out but, more often than not, they would eat at her apartment or his house, simply enjoying each other's company. At weekends he drove them out into the country, finding lovely little hotels to stay in, from where they could take long, leisurely walks.

At times Aimi felt as if she must be dreaming, for she was having much too much fun. Yet how could she help it, when Jonas was such fun to be with? She found that with him she could relax. It was a monumental relief to just be herself, and she would always be grateful to Jonas for giving her that.

Sometimes, though, she would catch sight of herself in the mirror when she was getting ready to go out, and be unable to look herself in the eye. Those nights her dreams would be troubled, and she would wake in the morning and know from her heavy eyes that the nightmares had visited her. It would take a concerted effort to act as if nothing had happened. Jonas never asked, but she knew he knew. He was waiting for her to make the first move, but she never would. Eventually the mood would pass, and she would be all right until the next time. What troubled her was that the next time was always sooner than the last.

She wasn't thinking about that now, as she lay with her head cradled on Jonas's shoulder, listening to him breathe as she waited for him to wake up. It was hot already, but the heatwave that had almost melted the country just weeks ago had broken eventually, to the tune of spectacular thunderstorms, returning them to a more normal heat of summer. They were in Jonas's bed, and through the open window she could see birds flying in and out of the trees.

Her pillow took a deep breath and she glanced round and up, her green eyes meeting sleepy blue ones. 'Good morning,' she greeted softly, liking his dishevelled look.

Jonas combed a hand through his hair and sighed. 'What time is it?'

'A little after half past nine,' she told him, taking a quick look at the clock on the bedside table.

'That late? You should have woken me,' he chided, but Aimi shook her head.

'I enjoy watching you sleep,' she confessed, and one eyebrow quirked as his lips twitched.

'Do you now? And how often does this happen?' he asked, shifting slightly so that he could run his hand caressingly over the lissome curve of her back and hip.

Her body stirred at his touch and she made a tiny purring sound in her throat. 'Only now and again.'

'Well, next time it happens, wake me. That way we can both enjoy the moment,' he suggested, lowering his lips to hers and taking them in a long, slow, deeply erotic kiss.

One thing led to another and it was quite some time before they were both capable of rational thought again. Later they shared the bathroom, Aimi showering whilst Jonas shaved. She was humming to herself, rinsing off the soap, when she thought she heard him speak. Turning off the tap, she opened the door a crack.

'Did you say something?'

Jonas looked at her in the shaving mirror. 'Uh-huh. Paula rang me yesterday to invite us out to dinner. I meant to tell you last night, but we got a little distracted,' he added with a wicked grin.

For once the look didn't register with Aimi; she was concentrating on what he had said. 'Did you say "us"?' she queried, reaching out for the fluffy bath sheet and quickly wrapping it around herself.

His eyebrows rose at her tone. 'What's wrong? Apparently she tried to contact you at home and, when she couldn't, rang Nick. He told her to talk to me.'

Aimi's heart sank and she stepped out of the shower. 'Oh, no,' she exclaimed in dismay. 'Why did he have to say that?'

Jonas went still, the hand holding the razor dropping as he slowly turned to face her. 'Why shouldn't he?'

'Because Paula isn't a fool. She'll realise that you and I are seeing each other!' Aimi explained in frustration, failing to see the odd look that flickered in his eyes for a moment. She had wanted to keep their affair from the other members of his family. Once it was public, it became real, and she could no longer ignore that reality.

'Are you ashamed to be connected with me, Aimi?' he asked her in a strangely level tone, and she belatedly realised how her remark must sound to him.

'No, no! That wasn't it at all!' she insisted, crossing to his side and touching his arm. How could she explain that their relationship was something she had entered into at great personal cost? She had broken faith with Lori to have this, and she knew it was that which troubled her sleep. She was being torn, and going public would not make things easier. 'I just wanted to keep it our secret.'

He shot her a dubious look. 'Well, Nick knows, and that didn't surprise you, so I assume you must have told him,' he pointed out reasonably, and she sighed.

'I didn't tell him; he guessed. He warned me against getting involved with you right from the beginning, and I made a mess of trying to pretend it wasn't you who sent me the rose,' Aimi explained quickly.

Jonas dropped his razor into the water and drew her into his arms. 'Well, you're right about Paula; she will have made the connection, which means the cat is very much out of the bag. So you're left with two options. Either you sit at home squirming, or you face her head on. What's it to be?'

Aimi might not have wanted to make their affair public knowledge, but if Paula knew the truth there was no point in hiding it. The damage was already done. 'What time do we have to be there, and should I wear a posh frock?' she asked by way of an answer, and Jonas's rakish grin reappeared like magic.

'Saturday, eight-thirty. I've not been to the place but, knowing Paula, it's bound to be expensive, where they do dinner and dancing. A posh frock is definitely required.'

Aimi smiled up at him, then, going on tiptoe, dropped a kiss on his nose. 'I'll go shopping for one during my lunch hour,' she promised and wriggled out of his hold before he could stop her. Laughing, she hurried into the bedroom, hearing him chuckling behind her.

Her smile faded, though, as she sat on the bed to dry off her hair. Suddenly she felt as if a shadow had fallen on the happy cocoon she had been living in, and she shivered as if a chill had passed over her. Immediately she told herself not to be so fanciful. Though she would much rather Jonas's family didn't know about them, there was nothing she could do about it now. There might be a few moments of embarrassment, but that would pass. Really, thinking about it, she was amazed that they had been able to keep the secret this long.

Yet, in the deep recesses of her mind, she couldn't shake off the feeling that something bad was going to happen.

When Saturday finally came around, Aimi paid a great deal of attention to dressing herself in the new dress she had bought for the occasion. She had treated herself to a pair of strappy sandals and matching evening purse, too. The deep blue of the dress complemented the soft blonde of her hair. After much thought she had decided to leave her hair down tonight, too.

Examining her reflection in the wardrobe mirror, she was almost amazed by what she saw. The woman who looked back was a stranger. An alluring, attractive stranger who didn't remind her of herself at all. Aimi was more used to seeing the cool, controlled person she had been these last nine years. This woman looked so much different from the young woman she had been before that. Of course she was older, but it was more to do with the way she held herself, with the confidence that only came with maturity.

Aimi couldn't help smiling a little, for she realised that she had been so busy she had failed to see she had grown up. More than that, she looked how she felt— happy—and that was all down to Jonas. At least, she was happy most of the time. She always felt that way when she was with him, but the bad dreams were getting her down, weighing on her mind when he was not there to distract her.

A glance at her watch told her that he would be here any minute. Even as she was thinking it, the doorbell rang and she smoothed her palms nervously over her thighs before going to open the door. However, any nervousness she was feeling vanished the instant she saw Jonas in his dinner suit. He was…breathtakingly handsome in the silk suit and all at once her heart was bombarded with all sorts of emotions, none of which allowed her to utter a word.

Jonas, on the other hand, had no such trouble.

'Stunning!' he declared when he saw her. 'I'll be the envy of every man in the room.'

'And I'll be the envy of every woman,' Aimi responded, finally managing to get her voice to work.

'I'm glad you left your hair down,' Jonas observed as he stepped inside. Carefully taking her into his arms, he kissed her and, like magic, Aimi forgot about her fears. When he drew back, he smiled gently. 'Nervous?'

'A little.' Whilst Aimi got on well with Paula and Nick, she couldn't help feeling neither would be happy that she was involved with their brother.

'Well, don't be; you're with me, so you can relax and enjoy yourself.'

Aimi stared up at him solemnly, then nodded. 'I'll do my best. You must think I'm ridiculous, worrying about what they will think,' she added with a wry laugh.

'Not at all. I've had my own worries,' he confessed, and she looked sceptical.

'You?'

Jonas shrugged. 'It's not easy to think seriously about a woman when you know that most of those who go out with you do so only because you're rich. After a while you start to wonder if they see you or your wallet.'

'I never thought of that. It must be unpleasant,' she responded sympathetically.

'It was, until you came along, and I realised here was a woman who saw my wealth as a turn-off. Naturally, I was intrigued,' he told her, eyes full of gentle humour.

'I've met a lot of rich men, and it didn't take me long to realise it's no measure of decency,' Aimi confirmed, thinking back to the world of the rich and famous she had once inhabited.

'And just where did you meet this horde of rich men?' he asked her teasingly.

Aimi dropped her gaze and moved away from him, ostensibly to collect her evening purse which lay on the coffee table. 'In another life,' she responded uncomfortably, not wanting to go there. Finally she turned back to Jonas and smiled. 'Shall we go? We don't want to be late.'

Jonas remained where he was, studying her broodingly. 'You'll tell me one day,' he said gently and her heart leapt, for it had been a while since he had mentioned her demons.

'There's nothing to tell and, even if there was, it's none of your business,' she told him firmly, which only made him smile grimly.

'I'm hoping that one day you'll trust me enough to make it my business,' he responded, stepping away from the door so that she could precede him out of it.

'Why would I do that?' she asked with a frown, watching him pull the door closed, then take her arm.

'Darling, the answer to that will be obvious when the time is right,' he told her lightly, hardly making things clearer so far as Aimi was concerned.

Aimi was puzzling over that very odd remark when they walked out of her building and she discovered Jonas had a taxi waiting for them.

Immediately Aimi started thinking ahead to the moment they entered the nightclub. She realised she was going to be making quite an entrance, and that set the butterflies fluttering around in her stomach. All eyes would be upon her, because she was with Jonas, and being the centre of attention was something she had become unused to. After all this time, she wasn't looking forward to it.

Strangely enough, though, when she did walk into the nightclub on Jonas's arm, she felt quite amazingly calm. Yes, people looked at them, some even seemed to recognise Jonas, but after that the attention faded away, leaving Aimi feeling a little bemused.

As if he felt something of what she was experiencing, Jonas glanced round, placing his free hand over hers. 'OK?' he asked, and her smile blossomed naturally.

'Yes…yes, I am!' she responded, and he grinned back at her before giving his attention to the waiter who was leading them through the crowded tables.

Paula was already smiling when Aimi and Jonas reached the table, and it was so warm and welcoming that Aimi forgot to be embarrassed.

'My goodness, Aimi, how lovely you look!' Paula exclaimed, rising and rounding the table to give her a friendly kiss on the cheek. 'Oh, dear, that didn't come out right, but you know what I mean!'

Aimi laughed. 'I do, and thank you, Paula. I love your dress.'

There followed a swift round of greetings and, in the midst of it, nobody but Aimi appeared to notice that Nick's response to Jonas was brusque at best. She had thought Nick was coming to terms with their relationship, but she could see that he was still angry with his brother, and that saddened her.

When they were all seated again, Paula leaned forward, her expression even more animated than usual. 'Isn't this a marvellous place? We've been sitting here name-spotting, and it's enough to make your head spin! Who have we seen? Let me see.' She began to relate a list, ticking them off on her fingers as she went.

'Did you get any autographs?' Jonas teased her, and she pulled a face.

'No. I was thinking about it, but James wouldn't let me,' she responded, shooting her husband a mock glare, then something caught her eye and she sat up straighter. 'Oh, my goodness, you'll never guess who just walked in!'

'Don't tell me, it's the Pope,' James quipped indulgently and received a kick for his pains.

'Don't be silly, he's in Rome. No, it's that fantastic actress. Ooh, you know!'

'I haven't the foggiest idea,' James told her, and Paula tutted.

'It's on the tip of my tongue. She gets all those fabulous meaty roles that make me weep buckets! I've got it. Marsha. Marsha Delmont!' Delighted at having made the connection, she beamed at everyone around the table.

Aimi looked round quickly, attempting to spot her mother, but the room was buzzing with people, making it difficult to see. 'Where?'

'She's gone,' Paula answered disappointedly. 'No, there she is, over the other side of the room.'

They all turned to look, and this time Aimi caught sight of the familiar figure of her mother. She smiled as a wave of pleasure swept over her. Her mother had been filming in New Zealand for the past three months, and she had missed her. She could see other heads turning, for Marsha Delmont was something of a national treasure. It was always the same wherever she went, and her mother responded with a small, friendly wave before she sat down.

It was then that Jonas, who had been looking across the room, turned to study Aimi intently. Almost at once she saw a look of comprehension enter those fascinating blue eyes and knew that he had discovered the answer to the mystery of who she reminded him of. Before he could say anything, though, the waiter, who had been hovering to one side, took their order for drinks and departed.

Opening her menu, Aimi knew it was only a matter of time before Jonas brought up the subject of her mother. She knew she should have told him, but she hadn't wanted him to make the connection, because then he could have remembered how her mother had rushed to be with her after the tragedy. She knew now that she didn't want him to think badly of her, although she knew he must. Who could think anything else?

The words of the menu blurred before her eyes as a profound question occurred to her in that moment. Why should she worry so very much about what he thought? The answer came shockingly loud and clear. Because a woman wanted the man she had fallen in love with to think only the best of her.

Aimi's lips parted on a tiny gasp as her true feelings were emblazoned in her heart and mind. She was in love with him. How could she not have known it before now? Because she hadn't been expecting to feel anything like this. Her affair with Jonas was just supposed to be a light thing, nothing so deep and momentous as falling in love. And yet she might have guessed it, because nothing about her relationship with him had been ordinary.

At that moment she suddenly became aware that Paula was laughing and looked up to find everyone at the table was looking at her. Having been miles away, she had totally lost the plot.

'What is it?' she asked and, across the table, Paula grinned.

'The waiter wants to know what you would like to eat,' she prompted and colour stormed into Aimi's cheeks.

'Oh, sorry,' she apologised and looked back at the menu, choosing the first thing her eye lit upon. The waiter made a note, smiled in a friendly fashion, then departed with the menus. Wondering what to say, she discovered she didn't have to when Jonas took her hand.

'Dance with me,' he urged her and, taking her agreement for granted, he stood up. She went with him for the simple reason that, if he was going to say anything, she didn't want everyone else to hear.

The dance floor was already crowded with couples and there was no chance of Aimi keeping some sort of distance from Jonas, even had she been inclined to, which, having discovered her feelings for him, she wasn't. He turned her into his arms, one hand settling in the small of her back, the other holding her hand close to his chest. Aimi placed her free hand on his shoulder, which brought her head close to his. Slowly, they began to move.

They had never danced together before tonight, and it was, quite simply, the most sensual dance she had ever experienced with a man. Their bodies touched from shoulder to thigh, and every gliding step she took brought with it the tantalising brush of his toned, muscular body. She was in love with this man was the thought going through her head, and consequently she made no attempt to stop her senses coming alive, registering every subtle nuance and sensation. Her body seemed to turn molten, softening, moulding itself to his in a way that stole her breath and started an ache way down deep inside her.

'It's crazy, isn't it?' Jonas murmured in a low voice next to her ear. 'That two supposedly intelligent people can't control the attraction they feel for the other, even in the middle of a dance floor.'

The provocative statement caused her to smile faintly and tip her head up so she could see him. 'You must be speaking for yourself. I have no trouble with my self-control!' she claimed flirtatiously.

Blue eyes danced. 'Liar,' came back his answer on a sighing breath.

Aimi stifled a moan as she felt the heat of his hand branding the small of her back. Dancing with him like this, knowing how she felt about him, was the most agonisingly sweet torture.

'You might not know me as well as you think you do!' she teased breathlessly, letting her fingers explore his neck and shoulders.

Jonas moved his head so that his cheek touched hers. 'I know you lied about not knowing who it was you look like,' he murmured for her ears only, and Aimi caught her breath, tensing a little. 'Why didn't you want me to know your mother is Marsha Delmont?'

Aimi closed her eyes momentarily, then bit the bullet. 'It isn't a connection I brag about, simply because my mother always wanted me to live out of the goldfish bowl she has to live in.' Although that hadn't worked, because Aimi had simply created her own notoriety. She crossed her fingers, hoping he knew nothing about her past.

To her relief, Jonas merely nodded. 'I can appreciate that. Now that I know, I realise where you get your acting ability from,' he declared, and Aimi laughed.

'I can't act my way out of a paper bag. It's my father

I take after. He was an academic. I get my love of history from him.'

'Beauty and brains. An irresistible combination,' he said with his devilish charm, and neatly turned her out of the way of a collision. 'Are you going to go and say hello?'

'A little later,' she confirmed, preferring to do it with a bit more privacy.

'Good, I'm looking forward to meeting her. There are some things I want to ask her about you,' he added, and her heart lurched anxiously.

'What sort of things?' she asked, her voice sounding unnaturally sharp, and felt the laughter in him.

'Don't worry; I only want to ask how she managed to produce such a beautiful, talented daughter,' he told her and, raising their joined hands to his lips, he pressed a kiss to her fingers.

Even so gentle a touch played havoc with her senses and brought a catch to her breath. 'Stop that!' she ordered huskily, though her attempt to pull her hand away was half-hearted at best.

'I can't help myself,' he admitted huskily, steering them over to the far side of the room. 'Whenever I'm with you, I have this urge to touch you. You haunt me, Aimi. My every waking moment is filled with thoughts of you, and my dreams…' He let the declaration tail off, knowing she would understand.

Aimi bit her lip hard, stifling a groan. 'Devil!' she berated him, but her eyes when she looked up at him were smoky with hidden passion.

'I've warned you about looking at me like that,' Jonas growled, and she smiled seductively.

'What are you going to do about it?' Aimi challenged, and he immediately stopped dancing.

'Nothing in front of all these people.' Casting a hasty look around, he found what he was searching for. 'Come with me,' he commanded, and took her by the arm to urge her through the tables to where French windows opened on to the night air. Her heart started to beat just that little bit faster.

However, they had only gone a few paces on to the terrace when a voice halted them.

'Aimi?' The soft question was comprised of hope and uncertainty.

At the sound of it, Aimi came to a halt and turned back to face her mother, who blinked rapidly, then sent out a beaming smile.

'I thought it was you!' she exclaimed, closing the distance in no time and sweeping her daughter into a tight hug. Aimi hugged her back, as ever inordinately glad to see her.

'I thought you were still away on location. When did you get back?'

Marsha Delmont laughed. 'Actually, darling, I'm not really back. Adrian broke a leg and is out of the production, so I've come home for a few days whilst a replacement is found. It's all too frustrating, but at least it gives me the opportunity to see you. Let me have a good look at you,' she said, and stepped back to put Aimi at arm's length. What she saw had her eyes widening in astonishment. 'Oh, my goodness!' She had to let go of her daughter's hands in order to bring them to her face. Tears spilled out down her cheeks. 'You don't know how long I've waited to see you like this! Oh, darling, thank God! I've been so very worried, but look at you. Your hair…your clothes… It's…absolutely wonderful!' More tears fell until Marsha was virtually sobbing.

Stricken to realise from this reaction just how concerned about her her mother had been, Aimi quickly gave her another hug. 'Don't cry. Please don't cry,' she urged, feeling wretched.

Marsha eased herself away and sniffed. 'I'm OK, darling. You know how emotional I get. Now I'm sure I had a tissue in here,' she declared, searching through her evening purse.

'Use this,' Jonas suggested, holding out a pristine handkerchief.

Taking it, Marsha used it to dab at her eyes, then took a good look at the man who had come to her rescue. Her eyebrows rose, and then she smiled. 'Now I understand,' she said knowingly, looking from Jonas to her daughter. 'Whoever you are, I am so very, very pleased to meet you!'

'Jonas Berkeley, Miss Delmont, and I'm honoured to meet you,' Jonas introduced himself with a smile, giving Aimi's mother a taste of his rakish charm.

'Marsha, please,' the older woman invited. 'And let's not stand upon ceremony. When I'm with my daughter I'm her mother, not an actress. If you're responsible for this transformation, then I'm in your debt.'

'Mum!' Aimi exclaimed in dismay, but her mother merely turned and smiled at her with so much love it brought a lump to her throat.

'Darling, I've waited so long for this day, don't try to stop me enjoying it.'

Aimi bit her lip. She knew what her mother was thinking, and she had to put her right. For, whilst she might have fallen for Jonas, she very much doubted he felt the same way. 'Mum, Jonas and I...we're not...'

Marsha laughed delightedly and cupped her daughter's cheeks. 'Darling, I don't care what you are or aren't, just be happy. Now, much as I would love to stay and chat with you for hours, I must go. Come and see me. I'm here until the end of next week. Bring Jonas. I absolutely insist upon it!' she added with another tinkling laugh, then kissed her daughter, smiled at Jonas and went back inside.

'Your mother is a truly lovely person,' Jonas remarked as he came to join Aimi, who looked up and smiled.

'I think so.'

'She's right about you, too. You look amazing, but that has nothing to do with me.'

Aimi knew better. He had a lot to do with how she was today. 'You're wrong. I would never have gone out and bought a dress like this but for you, and she knows it.'

Jonas turned her into his arms and brought her up against him. 'And are you happy?'

Aimi hesitated a moment, not because she wasn't happy but because it was such a difficult thing for her to say. To admit it would be a further renunciation of her friend. And yet...how could she not say it when, for the first time in so very long, she actually was deeply happy. 'Yes,' she admitted huskily, 'I am.'

He smiled. 'Good. That makes two of us,' he told her softly, and kissed her with exquisite gentleness.

Aimi rested her head on his shoulder, unable to stop

herself experiencing a new wave of guilt. Yet no sooner had the thought come, than she forced it back, not wanting to think about it now. She would only think of this moment, and no further.

They stood like that for an age, until another couple came from inside, breaking the mood.

'We'd better go and join the others. They'll be wondering where we've got to,' Jonas proposed as he released her, and immediately she missed the warmth of his closeness and its ability to fend off unwanted thoughts. He did hold her hand as they made their way back inside, but Aimi felt the cold winds of her past following in her wake.

No sooner had they reached their table than Nick jumped to his feet. 'Can I have a word with you?' he asked his brother in a surprisingly stern voice. Jonas's brows rose as he settled Aimi in her seat. Squeezing her shoulders encouragingly, he nodded.

'Of course, Nick. We won't be long,' he said to Aimi and the others, then turned to follow a rigid-backed Nick to the side of the room.

Not surprisingly, the others were intrigued by this turn of events and watched the distant conversation with as much interest as Aimi. It was clear to see that Nick was furiously angry, gesticulating wildly as he harangued his brother. Jonas simply stood and listened to it all. However, when Nick stopped for breath, he held up his hand and started to speak. Whatever he said, the change in Nick was profound. His posture softened and, as he listened, he dragged a hand through his hair. Then he had a question or two to ask and, when Jonas nodded, he hesitated for a moment, then held out his hand. Jonas took it, and they hugged. Seconds later, both men walked off in the direction of the bar.

'Well!' exclaimed Paula, looking from her husband to Aimi. 'That was interesting. What on earth do you think was going on?'

Aimi was frowning, wondering the same herself. 'I have no idea.'

'I know Nick didn't like you and Jonas being gone so long. Would it be too indelicate to ask what you were doing?' Paula's expression was part grimace and part wheedling as she looked at Aimi.

Aimi couldn't help laughing, whilst Paula's husband groaned aloud. 'Honestly, Paula!'

'It's OK,' Aimi responded. 'Actually, we were talking to my mother.'

Of all the things Paula had been expecting to hear, that wasn't one of them. 'Your mother!'

There was nothing else Aimi could do than come clean. 'Marsha Delmont is my mother,' she confessed, and Paula's face was a picture.

'Oh, my goodness! Really? Oh, Lord, did I say anything nasty about her? I did, didn't I? Oh, I just want to curl up and die!' she exclaimed, covering her face with her hands.

Aimi smiled understandingly. 'It's OK, Paula. You were very polite. My mother will be glad to hear she has another fan.'

'And I do like her. I really do!' the young woman declared earnestly. 'Now, spill the beans—tell us what it's like, growing up the daughter of a screen goddess.'

Amused and diverted, Aimi spent the few minutes until the men returned relating a few of the funnier episodes in her life. When Jonas finally took his seat beside her, she looked at him curiously.

'What were you and Nick talking about?' she asked immediately.

'He wanted to tell me what he would do to me if I harmed a hair on your head,' Jonas enlightened her with a wry smile, and Aimi caught her breath.

'I hope you told him to mind his own business,' she returned sharply. Employer or not, he had no right to interfere in her private life.

'Actually, I told him that if I ever did, then I would save him the trouble and do it myself.'

Aimi stared at him in a state of bemusement. 'Really?'

Jonas nodded. 'Really. I've come to realise that if there is one person in all the world I would never want to hurt, it's you. The simple truth of the matter is, I've fallen in love with you, Aimi Carteret.'

CHAPTER NINE

IT STARTED as it always did, with her whole body feeling the vibration. Then came the awful moment when she turned and saw the huge cloud of snow billowing its way downhill towards her. She couldn't move, no matter how much she struggled. Her heart was thundering sickeningly fast and, just when she thought it must burst, the picture changed and she was in the trees, watching. Watching Lori going the wrong way, trying to get out of the path of destruction. She tried to call out to her to hurry. *Hurry!* But the dreadful noise took her voice away, and she could only watch. Watch as Lori was swept up and tossed around like a rag doll, until she vanished from sight. Then the noise was gone and, where Lori had once been, there was only metre upon metre of uneven snow and debris. Horror gripped her as she realised her friend was gone, and she cried out against it. *No. No.*

'No!'

Now Aimi was trying to battle her way over the snow, but it was stopping her, fighting to keep her where she was, and she flung out wildly with her arms and legs until slowly a voice began to intrude.

'Wake up. Aimi, wake up. Don't fight me. Hush now. Hush.'

Slowly the snow that held her transformed into strong male arms and the voice she could hear was known to her, too. She subsided, trembling, looking up into familiar features.

'Jonas?'

He nodded and held her tighter, soothing her with the gentle stroking of his hand over her back. 'I'm here. I've got you.'

As reality impinged, Aimi realised she was sitting up in the bed and Jonas was beside her, his strong arms comforting her. 'What happened?' Her voice sounded odd, croaky and her throat hurt.

Jonas's heartbeat began to return to normal, too. 'You woke up screaming. When I tried to hold you, you started thrashing about. You must have had a bad dream.'

Bad dream? Aimi closed her eyes, knowing what had happened. She had had the nightmare again. These days she only had it around the time of the anniversary of Lori's death, but that was months away. She thought she knew the reason why it had come early, but then remembered something Jonas had said.

'Did I hurt you? When I was thrashing about?' she asked remorsefully, studying his face for signs of damage.

His lips twitched into a faint smile. 'No. I managed to get you in a rugby tackle. I thought you might hurt yourself.'

Aimi sighed and rested her weight against him. 'I'm OK,' she told him, though she wasn't really. She was still shaking. The nightmare never went away easily, but stayed with her for hours afterwards. 'I'm sorry I woke you.'

Jonas pressed a kiss to her temple. 'I'm more concerned about you than of losing sleep. What was the dream about?'

'I can't really remember. It's hazy and jumbled.' Again she lied, but she had never told anyone about her nightmares. They were too raw. Too private.

'You seem to be having quite a few bad dreams lately. Is something bothering you?' The concerned question set the nerves in her stomach jangling.

'No, it was just a random event. I have to use the bathroom,' she told him, wriggling out of his arms and scrambling off the bed. 'I won't be a moment.'

Once inside the bathroom, Aimi switched on the light and stared at herself in the mirror over the basin. There were dark shadows in her eyes, and she knew why. Two things had happened at dinner tonight. She had realised she was in love with Jonas, and he had told her he had fallen in love with her. It should have made her happy, and it had, yet the nightmare had come again.

Groaning softly, she ran some cold water into the basin and bent to splash it over her face. The cold felt good on her heated skin. Yet it couldn't take away the knowledge that she had been having more and more restless nights and uncomfortable dreams. It was as if the happier she had become, the more severe the dreams grew. Until, tonight, the nightmare had returned with a vengeance.

After weeks of being ignored, Aimi's conscience was raising its head over the barricade. It was no longer prepared to take a back seat. The moment she'd realised she was in love, it had risen up and tried to tell her something. But what? That she had taken too much for granted? That she had presumed too much? What? she asked herself, and her reflection in the mirror returned the taunting answer. *You know.*

Abruptly Aimi looked away, drying her face on a fluffy towel. She didn't want to think about it. Didn't want to acknowledge what her conscience was trying to tell her. She wanted to be with Jonas. Wanted to feel his warmth and know she was alive.

Without looking at herself again, she drained the water and switched off the light. Hurrying back into the bedroom, she slipped into the bed beside Jonas, who was resting back against the pillows, and held on to him tightly. Slightly surprised, he instinctively wrapped his arms around her.

'Are you OK?' he asked cautiously, and she squeezed her eyes shut.

'I will be. Just hold me, please,' she asked in a small voice, which for some reason made his heart turn over.

'Always,' he promised. 'Always.'

Aimi sighed heavily, praying his words would dispel the chilly sense of time running out that was growing inside her. Very slowly she began to relax and her breathing became more regular. To the man holding her, it was a sign that he, too, could relax. Then he heard the words he had been hoping to hear.

'I love you, Jonas,' Aimi murmured, very close to sleep, so that her words were slurred.

Jonas smoothed his hand over her silky hair. 'I love you, too, Aimi. Sleep now.'

At his words she uttered a faint sigh and slipped over the edge into forgetfulness.

* * *

The following morning Aimi woke before Jonas and from the second she opened her eyes she had instant recall of everything that had happened. She wanted to feel happy about Jonas telling her he loved her but, even as she thought it, she shivered. She couldn't help feeling that it wasn't right. That it was wrong to be this happy when her best friend had been denied the possibility of happiness.

Creeping from the bed, Aimi left Jonas asleep whilst she showered. She felt torn. On the one hand wanting what she could have with Jonas, yet on the other having this almost overwhelming feeling that she did not deserve to be given such a gift. The guilt over her best friend's death reasserted itself, weighing on her heart, turning the warm sunny day into something cold and dark.

Shivering, Aimi turned off the water and stepped out of the cubicle, drying herself on a large fluffy towel. Padding back into the bedroom, she quickly slipped into a pair of jeans and a long-sleeved lightweight top, then went to the kitchen and made herself some coffee. Whilst she sipped the steaming liquid, she noticed the small pile of mail she had tossed on to the counter the day before. A couple were bills, but one was handwritten, and Aimi recognised the writing. Setting the mug down, she picked up the envelope with trembling fingers and opened it.

Inside was a birthday card, and the sentiment in it was a stark and pointed reminder to Aimi. It said: *To our darling Lori. Happy birthday, with all our love, Mum and Dad.*

Aimi drew in a ragged breath, realising she had forgotten what day it was. Every year, Lori's mother sent

Aimi the birthday card she could not send her daughter, and it was as devastating to the recipient as it had ever been.

'Oh, God!' Aimi pressed a hand to her stomach, fighting back a wave of nausea. The timing was awesome, combining as it did with Aimi's own conscience reasserting itself. She was being assailed from all sides, and she knew she needed to get out into the open air where she could think.

Tossing the card on the counter, she headed for the front door. Yet she hesitated at the bedroom, staring down at Jonas's sleeping form. He had soothed her in the night, and she had felt safe from the ghosts of her past, but they had come back to haunt her anyway. Whilst part of her wanted him to hold her now, the other knew he could not help. She had to do this by herself.

So she turned away, collecting her bag on her way out of the door. At first her route had no purpose, except to take her away from the source of her present dilemma, but having done that, she slowed down, eventually finding a bench in a nearby park where she could sit and collect her thoughts.

Aimi knew what she needed to hear. She needed to be told that it was OK for her to have Jonas. But Lori was the only one who could give her that permission, and it was beyond her. Maybe she wasn't being rational, but she never could be. Not about what she had done. If Lori were here... But she wasn't—only her parents were.

Aimi sat up straighter, drawing in a ragged breath. Lori's parents. Mrs Ashurst had blamed Aimi as much as Aimi had blamed herself. Obviously she still did, from the card she had sent. But if she could just talk to her, try to explain what had happened, maybe she would be able to move forward. Find the true peace which was just beyond her reach.

Knowing now what she had to do, Aimi set off in search of a taxi to take her to the Ashursts' house. Her heart was thundering in her chest as she walked up to the front door. She had been here so often in the past, it had almost been a second home. Surely the friendly woman she remembered from her childhood would at least listen now.

Lori's mother opened the door herself and when she saw Aimi standing on her doorstep her expression froze, becoming tight and remote. 'Oh, it's you,' she said coldly, and Aimi's heart lurched. Still, she pressed on.

'Could I speak with you for a moment, Mrs Ashurst?' she asked the older woman, her voice gruff through a dry throat.

Mrs Ashurst's brows rose superciliously. 'What can we possibly have to say to each other?' she challenged, making no move to invite Aimi inside.

'Please, Mrs Ashurst. I need to talk to you about Lori. If we could just…' That was as far as she was allowed to get.

'Don't you dare let me hear you say her name! Lori's gone. You killed her!' The anger and bitterness were as strong as they had ever been, and Aimi felt herself begin to shake inside.

She swallowed hard and her voice faltered as she responded. 'I know I was at fault, and I'm sorry for it, but it's been nine years now, and I thought perhaps we could talk about that day.'

Lori's mother laughed scathingly. 'I know what you

thought, Aimi Carteret! You thought you could come back here and say you were sorry and then I would forgive you! Well, I don't forgive you! I shall never forgive you! You killed my daughter. She followed you like a slave and did everything you demanded of her! It sickens me to see you walking about free as a bird whilst she…' The woman faltered, dragging air into her lungs as she found she could not say where Lori was.

The older woman's face took on a vicious look. 'I don't care how sorry you are. It won't bring my daughter back to me. Go away. Get out. I never want to see you again!' And with that she slammed the door in Aimi's face.

Dazed and distraught, Aimi turned away and staggered down the steps. The other woman's venom was an awful thing to feel, and Aimi felt it slice into her heart, draining the warmth out of her along with the faint hope of being forgiven. Totally unaware of where she was going, she turned left out of the gate and simply walked. Her own sense of guilt expanded to encompass that which had just been levelled on her by Lori's mother. It weighed her down, almost as much as it had in the beginning.

There was no way out of it, and there shouldn't be. She *was* guilty. Nothing she had done could ever take that away. She had changed her life, become a better person, but that couldn't wipe away the blame. How could she even think of making a future for herself, with Lori's death on her conscience? Nothing could make that right. Lori's mother had proved that to her today. She didn't deserve the things that Lori could never have.

Lost in the labyrinth of her guilt-driven thoughts,

Aimi was unaware of anything around her. Not the people, nor the traffic. She just walked, and not even the sudden blaring of a horn could penetrate her numbed mind. Even the pain of the contact with the car which tried to avoid her but caught her a glancing blow that sent her spinning into a parked car barely registered. There was a scream which finally made it through the mist but, seconds later, all was blackness.

She seemed to be walking through a mist, on a surface she could not see. She knew she was looking for something, but it was beyond her sight, out of reach. She moaned softly, and almost immediately felt a hand holding hers. It was strong, yet gentle. It was instantly comforting and she relaxed, allowing the darkness to swallow her up again.

The next time Aimi stirred, the mists were gone, and she blinked her eyes open to the real world. It was night. She could tell that from the muted lighting that allowed her to open her eyes without discomfort. She had no idea where she was, or why, and when she tried to lift her left arm a dull pain shot through her wrist, so she quickly put it back down.

Somewhat alarmed, she tried moving her head, but she moved too fast and that set a dull pain throbbing inside it. Realising that she must have been hurt, Aimi tried all her limbs one by one, discovering she could move her legs and right arm, though not without pain. When she tried to sit up, the whole of her body protested, and she fell back against the pillows, gasping for breath.

She had to be in hospital, she realised, and a careful check to either side of her confirmed the suspicion. The big question, then, was how had she got here? What on earth had she done?

The question was silent but the answer was audible.

'You had a collision with a moving vehicle,' a familiar voice told her, and Aimi looked round to see her mother was standing just inside the room.

'I did?' Her voice sounded scratchy, for her throat was as dry as a desert. She couldn't remember having an accident, though right at the back of her mind she had the vaguest memory of a piercing scream.

'Yes,' Marsha Delmont declared wryly, coming to take the chair she had been sitting in for goodness knew how many hours. 'Apparently you stepped off the kerb almost into the path of a car. You were lucky. You got away with bruised ribs and a fractured wrist.'

That explained why her left wrist hurt. She tried to probe further, but that only increased the throbbing ache in her head, so she desisted. 'Is the driver OK?'

Leaning on the edge of the bed, Marsha took her daughter's hand. 'She's suffering from shock. As am I. You really must stop putting me through this, Aimi. My heart can't take it.'

'I'm sorry, Mum. I wish I could remember. Where did it happen?'

'In Chelsea, near the river,' Marsha revealed, and held her breath, but Aimi only frowned.

'What was I doing there?'

Her mother took a deep breath. 'Well, darling, it was rather close to where Lori used to live,' she said cautiously, and saw comprehension finally dawn on her daughter's bruised face.

The mention of Lori's name cleared the fog for

Aimi. She recalled where she had been, and why. 'I went to see her parents, but only her mother was there,' she said starkly.

Marsha's heart contracted. 'Why, darling?'

Aimi gave her mother a tired smile. 'I wanted to talk to them about her. It was…important to me. I thought… I hoped…that, after all this time, they would forgive me. I ought to have known they never will.'

Tears glistened in her mother's eyes. 'Oh, Aimi, Aimi, I'm so sorry you had to go through all that again. I tried to approach her several times in those first years, but she refused to see me. Maybe I would be the same, if I lost you. You have to try and understand how she feels, and not judge her too harshly.'

Aimi squeezed her mother's hand. 'I don't. I know she's right in everything she said.'

'What did she say?' Marsha enquired, not liking the sound of that at all.

'Only what I've always known, that it was my fault Lori died.'

'But Aimi, nobody blamed you.'

Aimi smiled wanly, not wanting to upset her mother any more. 'I blamed me. But don't worry, everything's all right now.'

Marsha was relieved to hear it. 'That's good, darling. Put it all behind you. You've been so much more like your old self lately, so I knew something had changed. It's Jonas, isn't it? He's a good man, and he's been so worried about you he refused to go home.'

Aimi froze. 'He's here?' She didn't know why she hadn't thought of that earlier, but her brain wasn't functioning properly yet.

'Of course. He's gone to get us some coffee. He'll be so relieved to find you've woken up at last.'

'Tell him to go away. I don't want to see him,' Aimi ordered bluntly. She knew why she had gone to Lori's parents, and that encounter had reminded her of what she had forgotten in the heat of passion. Jonas, and everything he represented, was out of bounds to her. She could not have the happiness she had denied her friend.

Not surprisingly, her mother was confused. 'But why? I don't understand. Has something happened?'

Yes, something had happened. She had stopped living an impossible dream. 'We haven't had a fight, or anything like that. I simply don't want to see him. Please, tell him to go home.'

'All right, if that's what you want,' Marsha agreed unhappily.

'It's OK, Marsha, Aimi can tell me herself,' Jonas declared evenly, and they both looked round to see him standing in the doorway, two steaming cups of coffee in his hands. These he set on a counter inside the door, then came further into the room. 'Would you give us a moment?' he said to her mother, who rose gracefully to her feet.

'Ten minutes,' she agreed, then, looking from one stony face to the other, sighed and left the room.

Jonas didn't take the seat Marsha had vacated, but stood beside the bed and slipped his hands into the pockets of his jeans. 'You gave me one hell of a fright. First I wake up to find you gone, then I get a call from your mother telling me you're in hospital. What were you thinking, stepping off the kerb without looking?'

Looking up at him, Aimi could see he was dreadfully tired and in need of a shave. Her heart ached, until she hardened it. 'I…had a lot on my mind. I just didn't realise the road was there. How long were you standing there? What did you hear?'

'Long enough to hear you say you didn't want to see me,' he enlightened her. 'How do you feel?'

'I seem to ache everywhere,' she responded, wincing as she tried to make herself more comfortable.

'That's because you're one huge bruise at the moment,' he returned with studied calm. 'So, why don't you want to see me, Aimi? What did I do to make you leave your apartment without a word?'

'I went out because I needed to think,' she told him curtly. 'And I don't want to see you because there would be no point. There's no future in our relationship, so the best thing to do is end it.'

That unexpected statement had his eyes narrowing. 'What do you mean, we have no future? Just last night you told me you loved me!' Jonas declared with justifiable disbelief.

Aimi swallowed hard. 'I lied,' she said gruffly, and he simply stared at her, patiently trying to understand what was going on.

'You lied?' Shaking his head, he dragged a hand through his hair. 'Oh, no, darling. I don't think so. If you've lied at all, it's now.'

Her heart lurched at the accurate claim. 'Why would I do that?'

Jonas uttered a derogatory bark of laughter. 'I don't know, but I sure as hell intend to find out!'

Aimi turned away from him, staring blindly at the wall. 'I'm tired. I want you to leave now. Please don't come back.' Although she couldn't see him, she could hear him take a deep breath.

'OK, I'll go, but this is not over. I'm not walking away from you, Aimi,' he promised, and she closed her eyes.

'You should. There's nothing for you to stay for. I can't give you what you want.'

'Then I'm doomed, darling because, so far as I'm concerned, you're the only one who can,' he responded, and turned and walked out of the room.

Aimi looked around, eyes fixed on the doorway he had just gone through. She knew she had done the right thing, but she hadn't thought it would hurt so much. It was as if someone had taken her heart and ripped it to shreds.

A movement in the doorway drew her from her painful reverie. It was her mother. Marsha crossed quickly to her daughter's side and sat down. Her eyes were full of concern.

'I met Jonas outside. He didn't look happy. Why did you send him away, Aimi? The man loves you. I can see it. Surely you must, too. Why are you doing this?'

Sighing, Aimi smiled sadly. 'Because I forgot about a promise I made, but I've remembered it now, so everything will be all right.' Her lashes fluttered down, and she heaved another sigh. 'I'm tired. I think I'll sleep now.'

Sitting back in the chair, Marsha shivered as if someone had walked over her grave. She had an awful feeling that she knew what her daughter was talking about, and it appalled her. She had been so overjoyed to see Aimi last night, looking radiant and happy, and she was determined that it would not be lost if she could help it. As soon as she could, she had phone calls to make and people to see. She was going to fight for her daughter as she had never fought before.

CHAPTER TEN

AIMI was not kept in hospital long, for her injuries had been blessedly minor—something of a miracle, given the circumstances. Jonas had not attempted to visit her again and she had been relieved, for she hadn't wanted to fight with him. He had stayed away, and she had done her best not to think about him. Through him, she had lost her way for a while, but she was back on track now.

Though she was allowed home, there was no way she could return to work. Nick had been extremely concerned about her accident and had insisted she take as much time off as she needed. She was grateful, yet at the same time had to wonder if she could still work for him. He was Jonas's brother, after all, and that was bound to create complications. Still, she wasn't going to think about it until she had to.

Her mother, who had delayed her return to work to be with her daughter, had come up with the perfect plan for her recuperation. She had been given the use of a cottage on an island in one of the Scottish lochs, and Aimi was going to stay there until she was fully recovered.

By the time she left hospital, she was longing for the

peace and quiet of the Highlands. Her thoughts had been anything but pleasant for, though she knew she was doing the only thing she could, her dreams were plagued with memories of what she had shared with Jonas and the possibility of what might have been. She had never been this troubled by a decision before and needed some quiet time to get her mind in order.

Marsha's driver took them to the station, where her mother waited to see her off, waving from the platform until a bend in the line took Aimi from sight. Aimi sat back in her seat then, knowing she had a long journey ahead of her.

Hours later, she discovered her mother had made arrangements for a car to take her from the nearest station to the loch, where a local man was on hand to ferry her over to the island. The same man helped to carry her cases up to the cottage.

'How will I contact you if I want to get off the island?' she asked him before he left.

'By phone. You'll find a number on the board in the kitchen. Enjoy your stay,' he added with a friendly smile, then walked back down the path. A little while later Aimi caught sight of him rowing back across the calm water of the loch.

Looking around her, Aimi breathed in a shaky sigh of relief. It was an idyllic spot, quiet except for the sound of birds and sheep in the distance. Though not big, the island was studded with trees and bushes, and there was a cottage garden all around it. Someone had put a lot of care and attention into it, and it was the perfect place to get away from her troubles.

She discovered, as she slowly unpacked her things,

that the cottage had all the usual appliances required for modern living—not that she would need them. She intended to live quite simply. By the time she had taken a walk around the garden, finding a shed with a generator in it, obviously for use if the electricity failed, it was late and she was getting hungry.

Back in the cottage, she made herself a sandwich and a cup of tea, and by the time she had finished both exhaustion was taking its toll. So, turning out the light, she locked up and took herself up to bed. She fell asleep almost the instant her head hit the pillow and knew no more until morning.

The next day was beautifully sunny and lifted Aimi's spirits immeasurably. After breakfast she decided to do a bit more exploring and, taking an apple with her in case she should get hungry, set off to walk to the southern end of the island. She was almost there when she thought she heard an outboard motor but, when no boat sped by, gave it no more thought.

Sitting on a rock in the sunshine, she ate her apple and watched the ducks go about their daily lives, hunting for food and chasing off rivals. Eventually, though, her stomach began to growl in earnest and she slowly made her way back to the cottage to make herself some lunch.

It wasn't until she approached the back door that her steps faltered. She had left it closed, but now it was open and she caught the waft of something delicious cooking. Noises followed, of pans being moved on the cooker. Her anxiety that somebody had broken into the cottage deepened to confusion at the idea that the same somebody was actually cooking.

'You might as well come in and wash up, the fish will be ready soon,' Jonas's voice called out to her from inside and anxiety gave way to shock.

'Jonas?' What was Jonas doing here?

Stepping inside, Aimi stared at the man standing at the cooker. He turned and smiled at her, and her heart leapt at the sight of him before she could stop it. She hadn't seen him since she had told him to go away at the hospital, and she hadn't realised just how very much she had missed him until this moment. Of course, as soon as she thought that, she forced herself to squash the emotion, to remain firm in her resolve.

'How did you get here?'

Jonas turned back to his cooking. 'I keep a boat at the dock. Jock looks after it for me. He also caught these fish. There's nothing like freshly cooked fish when you've been out in the fresh air.'

Aimi listened to the explanation in a state of disbelief. He kept a boat? 'How could you keep a boat here?'

'Because this is my cottage. My island, too, come to that. Look, make yourself useful and set the table. You'll find cutlery in the drawer over there.'

She was staggered, and knew her expression showed it. 'Your cottage? But I thought...' She never actually finished what she thought, for it dawned on her then that her mother and Jonas had planned this between them. 'I don't believe it! How could she do this to me?' she exclaimed, hurt by her mother's action.

Jonas took the frying-pan off the heat and turned off the gas. 'Because she loves you,' he answered simply, moving round and setting the table. Next he dished up the fish and vegetables on to two plates and set them on the table.

Aimi watched all this in silence. 'She had no right to interfere. I know what I'm doing,' she said stolidly, and Jonas shot her a questioning look as he came to hold out a chair.

'Do you? We'll talk about that later. In the meantime, the fish is getting cold, and it would be a shame to spoil it. Sit and eat, Aimi. You look like you could do with some food in you.'

She sat because she was too stunned to do anything else. The fish smelt wonderful, and her stomach rumbled. Telling herself it would be a crime to waste good food, she started to eat. Across the table, Jonas watched her for a moment, then started on his own food.

They ate in silence. Aimi couldn't have spoken anyway; her thoughts were too jumbled. Besides, she was still learning to cope doing things one-handed, and had to concentrate on cutting up her food.

'Does your wrist give you much pain?' Jonas asked after a while, and she had to look up.

'Some. I have painkillers but I try not to use them.' What with that and her bruised ribs, she sometimes felt like one big ache, but it was getting better, slowly.

'You've left your hair down, I see,' he remarked next, and automatically she raised a hand to her neck.

'I can't put it up with one hand,' she admitted, and it had left her feeling far too open. She couldn't even tie it back, so it had to fall to her shoulders in a blonde swathe.

'Now I'm here, I can help you,' he stated matter-of-factly, and Aimi stared at him.

'You won't be staying,' she stated as firmly as she could, but Jonas merely looked faintly amused.

'It's my cottage, remember?'

Her jaw tensed. 'Then I shall leave.'

Jonas pulled a face and rubbed his hand around his jaw. 'That might be a problem.'

Her heart lurched. 'Why? All I have to do is phone across.'

'The phone's been disconnected and, before you ask, there's no reception here for a mobile phone. You're going nowhere, Aimi. Not until we've talked this thing out.' He was no longer smiling. Looking into his eyes, she could see the steely purpose there.

'We have nothing to talk about. And I will get off this island, even if I have to swim for it!' she informed him, feeling anger coiling inside her at the trap she had walked into.

'How far do you think you would get with that wrist? We are going to talk—sooner or later.'

Aimi pushed her plate away, her appetite vanishing. 'Then it will have to be later!' she exclaimed, and attempted to push her chair away by bracing her hands against the table. Pain shot through her wrist and she gasped, clutching it to her chest. 'Damn! Damn, damn, damn!'

Jonas had shot to his feet in an instant, rounding the table to squat down beside her. 'Have you done any damage? Let me see.' He tried to take her arm, but she twisted away.

'Don't touch me!' she gritted out angrily. 'This is all your fault! Why did you have to come here?'

'Because I love you, Aimi Carteret, and I don't intend to lose you without a fight,' he told her with simple honesty, causing invisible fingers to tighten about her heart.

Aimi glared at him, unaware that her chin was trembling as she fought with her emotions. 'Don't say that! I don't want to hear it!'

'You think you don't, but I know better,' he contradicted, rising to his feet again, and Aimi stared at him helplessly.

'Why won't you listen to me?'

Jonas uttered a wry laugh. 'Because you haven't said anything I want to hear yet.' He collected up the plates, put the scraps in the waste bin, then piled them in the sink. 'Why don't you go and sit in the other room, whilst I make a cup of tea?' he suggested, setting Aimi's teeth on edge.

'Why don't you stop telling me what to do?' she retorted and, whilst she did get up, she stomped out of the cottage instead of into the sitting room.

She had no real idea of where she was going, just so long as it was away from Jonas. How dared he do this? It was her life, and she could choose to live it her way. *Even if it's not the way you really want...?* an insidious voice asked, and she hated herself for thinking it.

Pursued by her inner thoughts, if not Jonas, she walked on, going towards the other end of the small island. It was as she walked that she recalled what Jonas had said. He had a boat which he'd used to get here. Which meant it had to be moored somewhere close by. If she could find it, then she could use it to leave.

Spurred on by the idea, she followed what appeared to be a path that took her down to the rocky shoreline. From there she picked her way round the rocks and pebbles, until she saw what she was looking for. A boat-house had been built over a small inlet, and it was this she made her way over to. As she approached, she could see a padlock on the front, but guessed there had to be another way in. Rounding the corner in search of it, she stopped short at the sight of Jonas sitting on a large boulder, soaking up the sun.

'What kept you?' he asked blithely, and Aimi ground her teeth together in annoyance.

'I didn't know this was here,' she replied shortly.

'But you worked out that I had to have a boat some-where,' Jonas added, smiling. 'It's locked, but you can try it for yourself.'

She didn't even attempt to, for she knew he was telling the truth. Instead, she turned her back on him and stared out over the sparkling water. 'I'm tired of playing games. I want to get off this island.'

'I'll take you anywhere you want to go, providing you talk to me first,' he bargained with her, and she did look over her shoulder at him then.

'What do you expect me to talk about?'

Blue eyes bored into hers, the power in them apparent even at a distance. 'Lori. You can start by telling me about her.'

Shock tore through her at the sound of her friend's name on his lips. Her gasp was audible, and she knew she paled. 'Who told you about Lori?' she asked faintly, her voice sounding stiff and unnatural.

'Your mother. When you wouldn't see me, I paid a call on her. We had a long talk. A very interesting talk,' Jonas said in a firm yet gentle voice.

Aimi could feel her heart knocking against her ribs

as her anxiety level rose higher. 'I'm surprised you were interested.'

'Darling, everything about you interests me. The reason you do some things. The reason why you won't do others.' His choice of words had her throat closing over.

'What do you mean?'

Jonas got to his feet and crossed the uneven ground to stand before her. 'Simply this. It isn't that you don't love me. It isn't that you can't love me. The fact is, you won't allow yourself to love me. Why? You were prepared to, until the day of the accident. What happened? What did Lori's mother say to you that made you change your mind?'

Aimi was finding it difficult to breathe, she was so tense. 'It doesn't matter what she said,' she bit out tersely, but Jonas shook his head.

'Oh, no, darling, that's wrong. It does matter. Whatever she said turned you from the warm, loving woman I know you to be, into someone I barely recognised. Don't let her do it.'

She laughed, a harsh sound that made his blood run cold. 'Don't you get it? It isn't her, it's me!'

'What did *you* do?'

Aimi shook her head, closing her eyes against the remembered pain. 'I forgot.'

Jonas took her by the shoulders, expecting her to try and shrug him off, but she didn't. 'What did you forget, Aimi?' he asked softly, with all the precision of a skilled surgeon. 'That Lori was dead, or that you weren't supposed to be glad you were alive?'

To Aimi, hearing her secret thoughts voiced aloud,

it was as if a huge wave of cold water had washed over her, taking away all the oxygen. In the next instant, she took in a deep, rasping breath as if coming up for air.

'Why should I be glad?' she gasped faintly, shaking her head to try and clear it. 'Why should I be happy, when Lori's dead?'

'Why shouldn't you be?' he countered instantly, and she stared at him helplessly. 'How long is this penance going to go on?' Jonas asked next, taking the strength out of her knees, so they barely held her up.

'What penance?'

Jonas looked quite grim. 'Aimi, you've been living your life as if two people died on that mountain nine years ago, but only one did. I'm sorry your friend died, but you're alive, Aimi, and it's time you started really living again.'

'Don't say that!' she cried out, pounding her fist against his chest. 'Don't you understand? I killed Lori! I killed my best friend!'

'The avalanche killed her, not you,' he corrected in a flash.

Her eyes were wild with a mixture of anger and pain. 'She wouldn't have been there but for me! She always did what I said!'

Jonas's gaze bored into her. 'Then why didn't she follow you that day?'

The question confused her. 'What do you mean?'

'There was another witness to what happened, remember? You got to safety in plenty of time. If she had followed you, she would have been safe. Why didn't she?' He gave her a firm shake. 'Why, Aimi?'

Aimi blinked, trying to think. 'I...I don't know,' she said hoarsely, but Jonas wasn't having that.

'You do know. Lori didn't always do what you said, did she? Your mother told me she was a little spoilt and wilful. Why didn't she follow you?'

A picture flashed into her mind of Lori, not trying to ski to the other side of the avalanche as Aimi always saw her, but skiing down at an angle ahead of the boiling snow. 'She was trying to outrun it!' she gasped out at last. 'Oh, my God! Lori, you fool!'

The strength did go out of her then and she collapsed against Jonas, who gathered her up as if she weighed nothing at all. He said nothing more, but carried her back through the trees to the cottage, where he deposited her on the couch and wrapped a blanket around her.

'I'll make a cup of tea,' he said gently, running his hand over her hair before going into the other room.

Aimi could hear him moving about as she sat there in a state of shock. All these years she had lived with the knowledge of her guilt, and yet now she realised that Lori had been as much at fault as she had been. Neither of them should have been on those slopes but, when danger had come, Lori should have run for cover. She had had time. Instead, she had chosen to fly in the face of it, and had paid the price.

Jonas returned with two mugs of tea. He handed her one and she clasped her chilly fingers around it, needing the warmth. 'How do you feel?' he asked her as he sat at the other end of the couch, watching her carefully.

'Shaky,' she admitted. 'I'd forgotten what she did. I thought I was to blame.'

'That's what guilt does. You knew you were in the wrong, so you took on all the blame. Lori took a risk that day, and paid for it. But you've been paying for it ever since. It's time to let go.'

Aimi looked at him, tears welling up and running down her cheeks. 'How can I, when the original fault was mine? I should never have suggested we do it.'

'No, you shouldn't,' Jonas agreed softly. 'You were young and foolish, and the outcome was tragic. It may be the hardest thing you will ever have to do, my love, but you have to learn to forgive yourself. Until you do that, it really won't matter if anyone else does.'

A sob escaped her and more tears spilt over, tracking their paths down to her chin. 'How do I do that?'

'By being easier on yourself. By accepting that you're human and capable of making mistakes. By knowing that those people who love you will never abandon you, no matter what you do. I'm here for you, Aimi. There's nothing you can tell me that will make me love you less. It's OK to be alive, darling.'

Aimi cried then. Deep, racking sobs that shook her body. Jonas took her mug and set it down with his, then moved so that he could take her in his arms and hold her close whilst she let out all the sadness within her. Finally the tears subsided, and she sighed wistfully.

'I miss her,' she confided in a small voice, and Jonas smoothed his hand up and down her arm.

'Of course you do. She was your best friend,' he responded gently. 'Your mother said you never cried like this.'

'I couldn't. The tears just wouldn't come.'

'So you cried in your sleep, when your defences were down, instead.' He made the logical jump easily.

Aimi sighed again, feeling all the accumulated tension of nine years falling away from her. 'Probably. I don't really remember. All I knew was that I had to change. I wanted to be a better person. Someone I wouldn't be ashamed of.'

Jonas put a finger beneath her chin and tipped her head up so that he could see her face. 'You are a good person, Aimi. Never let anyone tell you differently.'

She caught his hand and brought it up to cup her cheek. 'I wasn't always. That's why I couldn't allow myself to have anything Lori couldn't. I didn't think I deserved to be happy.'

'No one deserves it more. You've done more than was ever required of you, darling. Nobody would deny you the right to happiness.'

She shivered as a shadow passed over her. 'Mrs Ashurst would,' she argued and saw a grim look set about his eyes and mouth.

'Lori's mother? I found a birthday card in your kitchen which must have come from her. How long has she been sending them?'

'Every year.'

Jonas looked as if he would like to do murder. 'My God, no wonder you were never able to deal with your guilt—she never let you forget, even for a moment!'

'Don't be angry with her. I never let myself forget. I just knew I had to make up for what I did,' Aimi soothed, touching his lips to stop the flow of words.

His expression softened as he looked at her, and finally he smiled and let out a deep breath. 'I'm angry because I almost lost you. You've more than made up for the past, Aimi. Now you have to look to the future. To us. Our happiness. Can you do that?'

She smiled back at him, at last allowing the love she felt for him to shine from her eyes. 'Yes. I've wanted to—so much. It was when I knew I had fallen in love with you that my conscience resurrected itself and stopped me in my tracks. Then the card came, and I was torn. I didn't want to lose you, but there was still my promise to Lori. I went to see her mother, hoping she would finally forgive me, but I guess she never will.'

Jonas shook his head. 'No, she won't, and she wants you to live in purgatory, too. But ask yourself this, Aimi. Would Lori want you to do that, or would she tell you to get on with your life?'

Aimi considered that, seeing in her mind's eye her friend's laughing face. Lori had always loved life, had been eager for the future. She would have urged Aimi to grasp it, too. 'She would have wanted me to be happy. To follow my heart.'

'Then that is what you should do, don't you think?' Jonas urged her to agree, and she nodded.

'Yes, it is.'

'In which case, I have to ask you a very important question. Will you marry me, Aimi Carteret?'

Looking deeply into his eyes, Aimi could see the hope and the fear he was feeling. He hoped she would say yes, but feared she might still say no. For her part, Aimi at last had no doubts. She might have moments of sadness over her friend but, with Jonas's help, she knew she would never again feel weighed down by blame. So her answer was simple.

'Yes, I will marry you, Jonas. How could I do anything else, when you've given me my life back, and I love you so much?'

Jonas closed his eyes for a moment and let out a heartfelt sigh. When he looked at her next, his blue eyes were ablaze with a quite stunning depth of emotion. 'Thank you. I'll make sure you never regret it.'

Aimi slipped her arms around his neck and hugged him tightly. She hadn't known this man long, but it felt as if she had always known him. He was the missing half that made everything right. 'I'm sorry I hurt you when I said I wouldn't see you,' she whispered in his ear, and one of the hands he had used to hold her rose to cup the back of her head.

'I think my brother and sister would tell you it was a lesson I needed to learn,' he returned wryly. 'The thought of losing you was…terrifying.'

'Well, you haven't lost me. I'm here for good,' she told him, easing back so that he could see just how much she meant it. 'I didn't intend to fall in love with you, but I'm so glad I did.'

His smile was half wicked, half sensual. 'Amen to that,' he agreed, and kissed her.

UNEXPECTED BABIES

One night, one pregnancy!

These four men may be from all over the world–
Italy, a Desert Kingdom, Britain and Argentina–
but there's one thing they all have in common….

When their mistresses fall pregnant after
one passionate night, an illegitimate heir is
unthinkable. The mothers-to-be will become
convenient wives!

Look for all of the fabulous stories available in April:

Androletti's Mistress #49
by MELANIE MILBURNE

**The Desert King's
Pregnant Bride** #50
by ANNIE WEST

The Pregnancy Secret #51
by MAGGIE COX

The Vásquez Mistress #52
by SARAH MORGAN

REQUEST YOUR FREE BOOKS!

HARLEQUIN® *Presents*~ ®

2 FREE NOVELS PLUS 2 FREE GIFTS!

PASSION GUARANTEED SEDUCTION

YES! Please send me 2 FREE Harlequin Presents® novels and my 2 FREE gifts (gifts are worth about $10). After receiving them, if I don't wish to receive any more books, I can return the shipping statement marked "cancel". If I don't cancel, I will receive 6 brand-new novels every month and be billed just $4.05 per book in the U.S. or $4.74 per book in Canada, plus 25¢ shipping and handling per book and applicable taxes, if any*. That's a savings of close to 15% off the cover price! I understand that accepting the 2 free books and gifts places me under no obligation to buy anything. I can always return a shipment and cancel at any time. Even if I never buy another book, the two free books and gifts are mine to keep forever.

106 HDN ERRW   306 HDN ERRL

Name	(PLEASE PRINT)	
Address		Apt. #
City	State/Prov.	Zip/Postal Code

Signature (if under 18, a parent or guardian must sign)

Mail to the **Harlequin Reader Service:**
IN U.S.A.: P.O. Box 1867, Buffalo, NY 14240-1867
IN CANADA: P.O. Box 609, Fort Erie, Ontario L2A 5X3

Not valid to current subscribers of Harlequin Presents books.

**Want to try two free books from another line?
Call 1-800-873-8635 or visit www.morefreebooks.com.**

* Terms and prices subject to change without notice. N.Y. residents add applicable sales tax. Canadian residents will be charged applicable provincial taxes and GST. Offer not valid in Quebec. This offer is limited to one order per household. All orders subject to approval. Credit or debit balances in a customer's account(s) may be offset by any other outstanding balance owed by or to the customer. Please allow 4 to 6 weeks for delivery. Offer available while quantities last.

Your Privacy: Harlequin Books is committed to protecting your privacy. Our Privacy Policy is available online at www.eHarlequin.com or upon request from the Reader Service. From time to time we make our lists of customers available to reputable third parties who may have a product or service of interest to you. If you would prefer we not share your name and address, please check here. ☐

HP08R

*Sicilian by name...scandalous,
scorching and seductive by nature!*

CAPTIVE AT THE SICILIAN
BILLIONAIRE'S COMMAND
by *Penny Jordan*

Three darkly handsome Leopardi men must hunt down
their missing heir. It is their duty—as Sicilians, as sons,
as brothers! The scandal and seduction they will leave in
their wake is just the beginning....

Book #2811

Available April 2009

Look out for the next two stories in this
fabulous new trilogy from Penny Jordan:

THE SICILIAN BOSS'S MISTRESS in May
THE SICILIAN'S BABY BARGAIN in August

www.eHarlequin.com   HP12811

HARLEQUIN *Presents*®

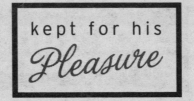

kept for his *Pleasure*

She's his mistress on demand!

THE SECRET MISTRESS ARRANGEMENT
by *Kimberly Lang*

When tycoon Matt Jacobs meets Ella MacKenzie,
he throws away the rule book and spends a week
in bed! And after seven days of Matt's lovemaking,
Ella's accepting a very indecent proposal....

Book #2818

Available April 2009

**Don't miss any books in
this exciting new miniseries
from Harlequin Presents!**